AN ELEGANT
EDUCATION

An Elegant Education

Meredith Leigh

Walker and Company
New York

First published in the United States of America in 1987 by the Walker
Publishing Company, Inc.

Published simultaneously in Canada by Thomas Allen & Sons
Canada, Limited, Markham, Ontario

Library of Congress Cataloging-in-Publication Data

Vivian, Daisy.
    An elegant education.

    I. Title.
PS3572.I86E44   1987   813'.54   87-14265
ISBN 0-8027-0974-5

Printed in the United States of America

10 9 8 7 6 5 4 3 2 1

For Ruth Cavin,
with gratitude and affection

AN ELEGANT EDUCATION

<h1 style="text-align: center">= 1 =</h1>

"REALLY, REDMOND, IT is too bad of you! The Lantrells have withdrawn Berniece, and the Willards appear to be about to do the same with Athena."

Her brother grimaced. "I expect they gave me as a reason, eh?"

Briony Mitchem shook her head sadly as she reread the two missives before her. "The letters are worded very discreetly, of course, but in both cases the reasons given are the same. The letters from their children have been far too full of the handsome drawing master. I daresay girlish rhapsodising has been the key, and they fear leaving impressionable young girls open to temptation."

Redmond's handsome, if now rather petulant, face clouded, and the young headmistress felt the warmth go out of it. "Dash it all, Bry, it is not my fault in the least. I have treated neither of those gels in any manner different from the others. I'll be swigged if I see how I can be held responsible for their silly crushes."

He rose from the armchair by the fire and flung himself angrily about the room. "You know, Briony, I really don't belong here."

"I know you don't, dear."

"I only stay on because I know you'd be lost without me to teach your inky-fingered young misses something about culture. It is a great service I do for you, you know, trying to drum some sense of the artistic spirit into the empty heads of the spoiled daughters of men our father wouldn't have seen fit to wipe his boots on. When I think of the use I could put that time to—time I waste on them—why, I fume! You've seen how my own work suffers because I cannot give myself up to it completely. I must always be thinking of your brats and how best to teach them something about drawing while fending off their romantic impulses."

At his sister's troubled look, the young man had the grace to check his tirade, but his expression was no less disgruntled. Briony, for her part, did not for a moment doubt his sincerity, for she knew from personal experience how trying it is to be the object of an infatuation, nor did she trouble to point out that Redmond was paid a very substantial salary for his labours. Her brother was very dear to her, and she had no doubt that he was an extremely talented artist. He was, unfortunately, not an eminently successful one. Redmond had an unparalleled gift for face-taking, but it was his downfall rather than his glory, and this for one reason alone: he took far too much pride in telling the truth. A ruthless or withered old merchant who had made his way in the world by clambering upon the backs of others did not want to be presented daily with an unmodified view of himself. Truth to tell, perhaps, Redmond was simply too good an artist for his own good.

As for the girls, well, perhaps Redmond could not help it. Females of all ages and persuasions had the habit of flocking to him, never for a moment put off by his often surly manner—more often obscurely excited by a male so elemental. But the fact remained that if he chose to continue as drawing master and accept his stipend, he must not let himself be tortured by the ignorance or the philistinism of his students. He must not think of it as a calling, merely as a profession.

Almost as if he had heard her thoughts, Redmond said, "What I really need is to get away, I expect." He held up his hand placatingly. "No, no, don't misunderstand me. I am grateful for everything you have done since our parents died. It is due to you alone that we have been able to keep our home, even in this situation, or hold up our heads in the county after the way father left his affairs when he went away to war.

"God knows, Bry, I only wish I had your head for business; I should be a great success if only I did. But there you are, you see. You have the brains, and I am left with only the genius." She understood that he meant it sincerely. He believed in himself above all else.

"It is a hard row," he added, "but we must live with it. I sometimes wonder if you have not made life too easy for me. The artist thrives on suffering, you see, and I have become indolent. I am like a well-fed cat purring by the fire when I should be starving in a London garret with only a crust of bread and a sip of wine to keep me going, eh? What do you think, Briony?"

She had listened to all this before; the plaint of the tortured artist was once again roaring through his head. "I don't know what I should do without you," she answered mechanically. But she knew very well. To take his place she would engage some quiet middle-aged drawing mistress— not too talented, not too intelligent, and one who did not ask for too much money. "Perhaps it will all work out," she suggested.

There was a discreet tapping on the door of the office and she made a little moue of regret, alerting her brother to the realisation that the world is too much with us, late and soon. He took the hint gracefully.

"Very well, dear sister, I shall try to be more discreet with the little vestals in the future. Perhaps I shall leave off shaving for a day or two or come to class with dirty shirt-linen. But no, I daresay it would only excite them more."

He pulled the door of the office open so sharply and with such force that the woman on the other side was tumbled into the room and flung into his arms. It was elderly Madame d'Artaud, the French mistress, and she pulled away with a little scream.

"Please, monsieur! Not everyone appreciates a . . . a . . . how do you say it in English, the *homme à bonnes fortunes?*"

Considering the conversation she had just completed with her brother, Briony could not contain a smile of genuine amusement. "In English one says that such a gentleman is a ladies' man, madame, but, I do assure you, your encounter was entirely accidental."

"Good gad!" Redmond exploded. "Do you really have the idea that I molest every woman with whom I come in contact? I *am* English, you know." He appealed to his sister. "Really, Briony, this is close to being the last straw! When the term ends, you may consider my employment at an end as well."

"Off to your London garret, are you? Do try for a north light."

He shook his finger at her. "You think I am joking, but when autumn comes round again and you have no one to become the butt of your jokes, I shall be exercising my art in the only way possible for a man of integrity."

"But you are still coming with me to Bath?"

"Not on your life, my sweet, nor even on my own. I leave you to swill down the dubious mineral beverage at your own risk. My prayer is that you do not make yourself ill by it."

His humor restored, he chucked the French mistress under the chin and propelled himself out with a flamboyant half-turn and bow, so that even Madame d'Artaud was forced to stifle a titter behind her hand.

"And now, madame, what may I do for you?"

It brought the French mistress quickly back to herself. "Oh, Madame Mitchem, you must forgive me, but your brothair ees so *amusant*." She giggled again, then recalled her mission.

"There is a gentleman, madame, waiting to see you."

Briony raised her eyebrows. Another disenchanted parent? "What sort of gentleman might that be, Madame d'Artaud? Am I expecting a gentleman at all?"

D'Artaud threw her hands in the air with an absurdly Gallic exaggeration. "Am I to know? You have not made of me the confidante in this matter." She held out a small bit of pasteboard. "He sends you this, a *carte de visite*."

Briony examined it. "And what have you done with this . . ." She looked at the card again, squinting a little to make out the elaborate Gothic script. ". . . this Graf von Ahlden, is it?"

"So it seemed to me, madame. I have placed him in the library and I have rung Melinda for refreshment. Is that well done?"

"Very well done, Vivienne. I do not know what I should do without you. Will you say to the count that I shall be with him presently?"

"*Oui*, I shall so say, madame."

She scuttled out, and Briony went into a small closet to bathe her face and wash her hands. It was a pity, she thought, as she poured the water into the basin from the earthenware jug, that this gentleman had chosen today to arrive without warning when she had been actively wishing that there might be no further upset until the term's end. She had no idea who he might be, but it came to her with a premonitory pang that trouble, or at least some sort of difficulty, attended him. She could not have said why she felt this, but the sense of it was strong.

Briony Mitchem was not a young woman given to extravagances of the psychic sort, but for the past few years she had almost come to believe that some sort of providence was keeping watch over her. She had survived many perils to come to where she now was. When her parents had died a few years since—first her father and then her mother quickly following—Redmond had still been too young to take on any responsibility, even though he was, in fact, the heir. It had come as a shock to them that the debts their father had left behind him when he went off to fight Napoleon amounted to more than the estate itself. When it was settled, there was little left save a large old house that no one wanted, sitting in the midst of an untended, over-grown park, and a small inheritance from Briony's grand-mother, which the creditors could not touch. Nothing more. Not enough, even, to remove to a smaller, more economical dwelling. And certainly nothing with which to send Redmond back to school, for his school fees were more than they had altogether.

On such a foundation was Mitchem Academy born. On the whole it had not been a rewarding experience, but it had kept them alive and had kept the house in repair instead of rotting down about their heads. There were always those, of course, who were willing to pay for the dubious privilege of lording it over a lady with an ancient name fallen, in their view, upon hard times. Not many of them, actually, for Briony did not permit it. Generations of breeding had ensured that Briony would have no intention of being intimidated by upstarts, had no aptitude for cringing, and no resemblance whatsoever to a small, grate-ful white mouse.

The parents of her charges, nevertheless, got good value for their money, and if they supposed that Mitchem Aca-demy and Briony's instruction would turn their darlings into silk purses, then let them pay. She was conscientious and made a point of educating the educable, but the silly and slothful were left to their own devices, unless she divined some spark within them. For the most part the system worked well enough. She gave her graduates a surface sheen, a patina of gentility, and sent them on their way. Sometimes she wondered what it passed for in their own circles. What became, for example, of the girls from Buenos Aires or Virginia, or even that one exotic bloom from Constantinople? Perhaps she had turned them into ladies, after all.

Now, as she moved through the house toward the library and her interview with the Gothic-lettered count, she thanked her stars that the term was nearly ended. It would be the first summer she had no señorita, no colonial lass remaining through the long vacation. She would be, for a little while, free as the wind. For the first time in many years she was returning to a favourite haunt of her childhood. Her dead mother had quite adored Bath.

As a resort for the unwell, or those who so fancied themselves, it had a solid reputation. It afforded all the amenities of the idle and well-fixed. There were lovely walks, there was a stream with river ambitions; there were concerts, cotillions, and assemblies; there were elegant lodging-houses and a rich array of shops surrounding the handsome old square and church. Some sort of activity, she recalled, was available at nearly any hour, and the games in the Lower Rooms opened early in the evening and closed shop near dawn. Not that she had been allowed to gamble, of course, though there were children younger than herself who did. She did not gamble now. Both Mama and Papa had suffered from that addiction, which was why everything had been lost.

Her time in Bath would be the first real escape she had had since the opening of the school six years past, and she planned to make the most of it, collecting enough memories to carry her through the dull routines of winter.

= 2 =

THE GENTLEMAN WHO awkwardly rose to his feet when Briony entered the library surprised her. Perhaps she had expected someone round and jolly, or perhaps even a desiccated and austere old Junker; it was not, in any case, this slim and aristocratic creature in grey cutaway and nankeen pantaloons strapped beneath his elegant boots. She noted on the table beside him an expensive wide-brimmed beaver, and the ivory-embellished cane on which he leaned sported a gold knob.

She put out her hand. "Good afternoon, your lordship. I am Miss Mitchem."

He clicked his heels and bowed as deeply as his infirmity would allow. "Count von Ahlden at your service, *Fräulein.*"

"Your servant, sir. Will you not be seated again?"

"Thank you." He did so with some difficulty, though without making a show of it. "You will forgive my clumsiness. I suffer from a small memento of our engagement at Bautzen a few years since."

Briony knew the Battle of Bautzen very well indeed. Bautzen was a walled cathedral town in Saxony, held against Napoleon's Army of the Elbe by Wittgenstein. It had been there that her father had given his life in a typically quixotic gesture, defending a city which had nothing at all to do with him, leaving all his burdens frivolously behind, sending her mother over the edge of depression into despair.

"Is that chair quite comfortable?"

"Thank you, it is very much so." He held a quizzing glass up to his right eye and surveyed her carefully in a manner that might have seemed rude had it not been done with a complete lack of artifice. She stared straightforwardly back at him with slightly raised eyebrows.

"Do you approve of what you see, count?"

"Forgive me, Fräulein Mitchem, if I appear outrageous to you, but from your formidable reputation I had expected someone rather more . . . mature. Someone rather more of a . . . of a dragon?"

He paused in momentary confusion. "Not an *old* woman, you understand, but hardly so youthful—and if you will pardon me saying so—so attractive as you are."

He stumbled again. "Am I saying this badly? My English is rusty, I know. Please understand that I do not mean to offend."

Briony could not help smiling a little at his discomfiture. "Parents are often taken aback at first meeting, Graf von Ahlden, but I do assure you that I have a number of years of experience to my credit."

"Ach, that I am aware of. You have come highly recommended as a woman of great patience and integrity; a woman well able to deal with, shall we say, *difficult* charges?"

A small inkling of what he perhaps had in mind began to dawn in Briony's mind. "You have spoken of 'reputation' and of 'recommendation,' sir; recommended by whom, if I may ask? I have had no experience except with rather ordinary girls."

He nodded as if he considered that a perfectly natural question. "I speak in particular of Lord Oxenard . . ."

"Ah, yes, Jenny's father."

"And of a Señor Perhuia," he continued as if she had not interrupted. "Both girls are companions of my . . . employer's daughters. I believe that both Miss Oxenard and Señorita Perhuia were with you for some time?"

She remembered both girls all too well. Jenny has been

as giddy as a butterfly and Estrella Perhuia had languished for the skies of Argentina for all the time she had been in England. Briony could, she supposed, take some small pride in them, since by the time they had left the Mitchem Academy they had been transformed into relatively normal young ladies of their class. Estrella had learned to carry on a simple conversation in either English or French, and Jenny appeared to have acquired at least a modicum of common sense—not much, mind you, but a measurable amount.

"I fear I cannot claim credit for more than some ordinary guidance in either case," she confessed. "Girls quite often grow out of small difficulties of their own accord."

His face fell. "I hope you will not disappoint me, Miss Mitchem. It it a matter of importance, and I know of nowhere else to turn."

The schoolmistress stirred uncomfortably, her vision of Bath rapidly receding. "I take it, sir, that you have a daughter or a ward in need of somewhat special attention?"

"Not my own daughter," he said, and she sensed that it was said thankfully, "but a certain young woman of good family who has been placed in my care. She is, to put it bluntly, someone who badly needs an opportunity to, as you have suggested, *correct* herself."

Briony sat very straight in her chair, vowing to be undefeated. "I shall be happy to discuss her enrollment in the fall term if you like. Perhaps the company of other young ladies will be beneficial."

He threw up his hands in patient agitation. "Oh, no, no, that would never do. She needs your care, your personal supervision!"

"I am not a jailer, Count von Ahlden, and Mitchem Academy is not a prison. I am sorry if your ward is a problem to you, but I have other plans to consider— personal arrangements."

He frowned, perplexed. "But your school term ends for the summer in a fortnight, I believe?"

"It does, and I mean to have an entire summer of complete relaxation."

The count hesitated as if wanting to speak, yet wondering whether to mention this next thing too soon. "I am empowered to offer you a substantial sum of money, Fräulein Mitchem," he said almost apologetically.

"I am sorry." She was firm, but the answer was accompanied by a gracious smile. "And, now, count, if you will excuse me?"

He held out a restraining hand, not touching her but allowing the gesture to serve. "Please, will you allow me a few minutes more?"

Briony shook her head. "I regret that my time just now is limited, Graf von Ahlden. Prize Day is at the end of this week, and we are not nearly ready for it."

"A *very* great deal of money, Miss Mitchem." He named a sum which made the headmistress stare. It seemed to her that he must surely be making fun of her.

"I cannot believe you are serious. Even if I were to devote my entire summer to your charge, I should not expect to be paid so much."

"Nevertheless, that is the sum I am instructed to offer, since you *would* be devoting your entire summer to the task. I further must make the point that the task would not be an easy one—rather more of a challenge than your well-bred English misses, I daresay, although I have every personal confidence in your ability to meet it. No, there is no question in my mind but that you would earn every pfennig of it."

Miss Mitchem's pretty chin went up stubbornly. "Nevertheless . . ."

Von Ahlden gave her an almost pitying look, though it had in it a great exasperation as well. "Do come down from your height, fräulein. I know exactly the state your finances are in. Your ledgers balance, but there is little left for carousing, I think. During your projected stay in Bath you will be living in cheap lodgings on a shoestring so fine as to be little more than a thread—and your handsome brother will one day run off and leave you."

"You seem to know a good deal about my circumstance," Briony said. "My brother has been making threats to do so for some time, but has never acted upon them."

"Would not, however, such a sum as I have mentioned be very handy in the pocket should he decide once and for all?"

"*I* would still not have had my holiday, however, and I have had none for several years."

The Graf von Ahlden seemed understanding of that issue as well. "It is true, you are certainly deserving of it, for you have worked very, very hard to make your school what it now is. You are to be congratulated on that score, but now I ask you—and I mean it without offence, please believe me—would it not be a pity to be an outsider looking on in Bath? Surely the amount you have arranged to put toward it would prevent you from attending all but the free entertainments and the outdoor concerts?"

Briony felt herself colouring. "Really, my lord, you go very close to the line."

His expressive mouth curved up into an enigmatic smile. It reminded her of that on the antique statue of Pan, which Briony had allowed to remain in the academy garden only because a lavishly foliaged vine had entwined itself picturesquely about it.

"What I ask is only this, dear lady: would you not prefer to spend your time in a *schloss*—how do you say, a country house?—with every convenience at hand and a staff fully trained to do your bidding, rather than mingingly on a poor street in a rich town?"

"Then you do not ask me to keep your ward here?"

"Ah, no. Your house can be closed for the summer, just as you had planned. It might even be better to allow no one to apprehend that your plans have been altered."

She eyed him severely. "Thus far, sir, my plans have *not* been altered."

The count opened his hand in a generous-minded gesture. "And then," he continued as if she had not spoken, "to spend a fortnight in your beloved Bath at the expense of . . . at *our* expense . . . and far more elegantly than you could have afforded on your own. Does that have no appeal?"

She had to admit that it did sound delightful, but she still knew less than nothing about his ward of about the requirements of her education.

"She is an interesting case," he said carefully. "Quite a challenge to any academician. A clever girl in many respects, but dull and stupid in other ways. She has, unfortunately, a predilection for the table and has consequently become rather gross. This has led to a virtual retreat from society. She needs, you see, to be quite made over."

"In two months' time?" asked Briony in surprise. "You expect miracles, I believe."

"Perhaps I have overstated a bit, but I do not wish to further intrude upon your day, Miss Mitchem, since you have so many other things to do. I will return, if I may, at a more convenient time. In the next day or two, shall we say? It will leave you time to turn the idea over in your head. Let us see if we cannot find a solution amenable to each of us."

Briony smiled wisely. "I know, sir, that you believe time will work in your favour, but I must warn you that it is not likely that such will be the case."

"Perhaps I do believe it. I think you are far from being a dull woman, and I know that the opportunity I offer is a great one in certain respects. It is certain to be a difficult task. You will earn your fee twice over if you agree to undertake it."

Very reluctantly she agreed to consider his offer. All through the night that amazing sum of money fairly danced in and out of her dreams, weaving a mightily seductive spell. But, oddly enough, the count did not return on the following day, nor the one after, nor even the one after that.

She related the story to Redmond, and he looked at her as if she were mad.

"An amount of money like that? Egad, Bry! Do you know what you could do with so much money? Why, when I think how long it would keep me in London! I could live a year on it! What is two months to you? My God, you're only two years older than I am, for all your airs!"

Briony suggested that she knew exactly how old she was, thank you, and she knew that long years stretched out ahead of her with endless lines of silly young girls waiting to be turned into proper young ladies. "I had rather expected support from you, Redmond. You disappoint me."

He had the grace to flush at that. "Oh, come, you know I love and respect you, no matter how feckless you are." She had to be content with such a backhand way of making amends.

By the fifth day after her conversation with the Graf von Ahlden, she had quite given him up and come to believe all had been a hoax or that he had changed his opinion of her capabilities. Not that she was even yet persuaded, but still she found she rather resented that he had held out the carrot, then withdrawn it.

And then, when she thought of the huge sum he had mentioned and what could have been done with it, she found herself becoming quite angry, though whether it was with him or with herself for not accepting the task in the beginning she did not know. She *could* have had a glittering respite from the dreary round, Redmond *could* have been supported for a year in romantic London penury—and there was the reputation of her school at stake, was there not? His nonappearance was, in fact, rather an insult. Had the Graf von Ahlden or his master (who must be, after all, a person of some consequence) been persuaded to withdraw altogether from the suggested arrangement? And how would that affect her future if such a thing should become known? It was one thing for her to have made the grand gesture of refusing them, but that they should have refused her, after all? Despicable.

All this, however, was not in the forefront of her consciousness, for Prize Day was upon them, and she had very little leisure to annoy herself over the matter. What was done was—regretfully—done. She had said no, the count had taken her at her word, and there was an end to it. Or so it seemed to her just then.

The day of the honours-awarding dawned with as bell-clear a sky as one could ask for, but before ten o'clock the day had become overcast and intolerably dreary. The girls in their white summer muslins looked apprehensively upward, although the platform had been erected beneath a large marquee on the lawn. In the event, however, everything went off well enough. Briony had not been too embarrassed, though it had been rather a shock to recognise that the poem written expressly for the occasion by the class laureate had been substantially cribbed from Alexander Pope. Luckily this was apparent only to Miss Mitchem and her mistress of history and polite literature and since the girl in question was leaving, it seemed politic to let the matter pass.

Redmond had been pressed into service and rather reluctantly gave the drawing prize to a young woman who so patently adored him that she stood quite enraptured in seraphic contemplation of his beauty rather than accepting her award. This provided a ripple of laughter and a much-needed lessening of tension amongst the audience.

The games mistress alone declined to present a trophy. "They are all ninnyhammers, Miss Mitchem, and I do not care to become a laughingstock among my peers. I really do not know why you have a mistress of mathematics and games at all. These young women have no energy and no heads for figures. There will also be no mathematics prize."

"That seems rather severe."

"I have my integrity, miss. Euclid would never forgive my apostasy."

It was after the last of the presentations when, amidst fairy cakes and punch, the parents and guardians were being trotted about the school, that Briony Mitchem was approached by a brawny gentleman with a distinctly up-country look about him and an accent to match.

"Mayn't I have a word with you, miss? I think I can say 'twould be to your advantage."

Briony, who had a great many calls upon her time today, nevertheless was intrigued by the man's earnest approach. "Even if it were not, sir, I should be happy to spare a moment for the father of one of my pupils." She looked at him closely. "Though I must confess I am not altogether certain I place you. Is it Rachel's father? I believe I detect something of a resemblance about the eyes."

"Nay, Miss Mitchem, I have no children here."

"Oh, a ward, then! Can you be Mr. Ainsley, Priscilla Fand's guardian?"

He looked rather uncomfortable, and she wondered if she had somehow put her foot wrong. Priscilla was, after all, not the most amenable of girls.

"I have no ward here, either, miss. I had no idea that today was different from any other or I might have chosen another time."

"Then, I fear, you have the advantage of me, sir."

She now looked at him more closely, rather pleased at what she saw. He was certainly not a handsome man in the conventional sense, but there was, even out of his own milieu as he appeared to be, a great vitality about him which she would have found attractive in anyone, male or female. He was nearly a head taller than herself, and she was not a tiny woman. Looking into his face for a resemblance to some pupil she had not passed over the fact that his jaw was very square and his crinkled eyes were very blue. She could think of at least two of the teachers in her employ who might well become quite flighty in his presence.

"I am anxious to discuss a bit of business, if you will lend me a moment?"

She looked about helplessly. "Ah, business . . ." She spread her hands as if to indicate how much call she had upon her time. "I wonder if today is quite . . ."

"A bit of money-bearing business, if you catch my drift, miss."

She wanted to smile at his persistence, but something in his manner quite forbade it. "I see," she said. "And your name is . . . ?"

"Barstow, if you please. Benjamin Barstow from Hawkshead up in border country."

"And you have it in mind to place a pupil with me?"

He hesitated. "Yes, I do in a manner of speaking."

"For this coming autumn, I presume?"

"Nay, miss, what I has in mind is to place a pupil with you for the summer."

Briony felt strangely as if she were reliving her life a day at a time. "Oh, but that is quite impossible," she said in quite the same way she had spoken to the count. "The academy, you see, is shut down during the long vacation. I shall be on a holiday of my own."

"Aye, I know all that."

"You do? Then why . . . ?"

There came into his face a surge of determination she had not witnessed before. "I need you, young woman, d'you ken that? And what I need I generally achieves on a matter of principle, tha understands. I can pay my way. It is no matter of charity."

But Briony Mitchem was beginning to become more than a little annoyed. First one and then another. How did it happen that these arrogant men, so different and yet so alike in their male stubbornness, could dare to suggest that she rearrange for their convenience her first holiday in years? Really, they were quite impossible.

"I think that if you had taken the time to write in advance

Mr. . . . ah . . . Barstow, is it? . . . you would have saved a rather long and, I expect, tedious journey."

He smiled as winningly as if her words had been real and not mere form. "Nay, you must not be concerned about that. I had business nearby. It was the mayor there that sent me to you, point of fact. Mayor Dedham seems to think highly of you and what you have accomplished."

"I am sure that is gratifying, but, you see, Mitchem Academy will be shut until September. The girls will be gone and so shall I."

"Aye, I understood that. But you *do* take summer pupils?"

"I have done in the past, but this year I am resting from my labours, you might say. If, perhaps, you would care to enroll your daughter for the . . ."

"Anne, her name is."

"If you would care to enroll Anne for the autumn term, I daresay it can be arranged. I can take a bit of time from the festivities now, if you like."

"Nay, you have missed my point. She would not fit in among your girls, you see."

Briony was puzzled. "Do you mean that Anne is handicapped in some way? I am sure the girls would not . . . "

"No, no," Barstow shook his head in amusement. "She is as rare a lass as you would think to see. A real beauty, you understand, but there lies the problem. She is too fine, you ken."

They walked across the lawn as they spoke, and Briony confessed her lack of comprehension. "Why, then, would she not fit in?"

He shrugged. "I have let this go too long, I fear. She is a bit older than your girls. She would not be comfortable among them children." Gesturing toward the young ladies and their parents, he conveyed the image of a spinster nearing middle age, though Briony suspected such was not really the case.

"But my young ladies often remain until they are seventeen, occasionally even longer."

"Yes, miss, I expect so."

"Your daughter is older than that?"

He caught the faint astonishment in her voice. "You have a right to be taken aback, but it is not the lass's fault she is behind, tha kens. She is educated, mind. She reads and writes and does sums like the very lightning, but she has only the manner and ways of her own class. My class, I admit, and I am not ashamed of my folk nor myself. I have done pretty well for a chap who taught himself everything, working all day at the foundry and studying by the light of the evening fire, but I want a bit better than that for my girl. I want her to move amongst my betters as their equal."

"But what if Anne does not want that for herself, Mr. Barstow? I think you underestimate yourself. I am certain your daughter had great admiration and affection for you."

"Oh, aye. I know that, but this part of it is not to be her decision. She is a good girl. She will do as I ask her.

"What I want for her, you see," he went on, "is that she *can* choose. I do not wish to hold her back, you see. She may go or stay, but to choose she must have a chance for choice. She must know enough of the rules of the world to take her own way, not mine. I do not wish her to make *me* happy. I wish her to be happy of her own self. Does tha follow me?"

Briony studied him with admiration. He was obviously a strong man in the physical sense. He had, as he said, been a worker who determinedly pulled himself up, but he had not allowed his success to soften him. It was also strikingly obvious to her that he loved his daughter very much and was acting out of a real concern for her and not a vaulting ambition of his own.

She walked along, deep in thought, wondering what she could say that would be of help to this caring parent which would neither offend him nor dampen that great enthusiasm for his daughter's welfare. At last she suggested, "If I could some time meet your daughter, Mr. Barstow, I could perhaps better advise you."

"I already know what I mean to do, miss. It is how to proceed with it that bothers me. I want my Anne to move freely amongst all folk, that is all."

"And you find that you do not?"

"Nay, *I* do. I do it because I have made my own way and among most folk I am respected for that. But for Annie, you know, it will be more difficult, strange to say. I can move pretty freely on my own, but Annie cannot."

"I can believe, sir, that you are respected no matter what people you are among, but without knowing your daughter, I fear I cannot understand your difficulty."

His craggy face brightened. "Aye, that is easily done. Can we see you in a day or two?"

"I fear I shall be gone away in a day or two. I meant, of course, in the autumn when classes begin again."

Barstow spoke patiently to her as if to a dear but backward child. "I fear you do not understand me. Autumn will be too late. We move into the hall in autumn, and Annie must be the mistress of it."

Now it was beginning to be somewhat more clear to Briony. It seemed evident that this upward-moving man had made his money and now wished to better his style of living. It might be that he had built himself a house, perhaps only purchased one such as Mitchem Hall might have become if it had not been metamorphosed into Mitchem Academy. Perhaps Anne Barstow was, even in her loving father's eyes, not yet capable of acting as mistress of such a pile, much less acting as Lady of the Manor, which might well be what he had in mind.

"Where is your daughter now?" she enquired. "I might spare an hour or two."

"She is at the Wild Swan in Hadrian's Green. We had . . . I had . . . business in the neighborhood. She travels with me often, you see."

Oddly, Briony did see, or rather she suspected something of their relationship. It had always been, she fancied, a richly interdependent one, but now that he sometimes took her along on his business journeys, he was beginning to see that the ways and manners she had learned along the border would not carry her through the rigours of society in the south. Seeing the gleam of expectant hope in his eyes, she raised her finger and shook it at him decisively.

"You must not raise your expectations, sir. With all respect, I have no intention of sacrificing my only leisure to your immediate need, but I may be able to put you in the way of meeting a substitute. One of my mistresses, perhaps, might do you very well indeed."

"You disappoint me, Miss Mitchem. Not yourself, then?"

"I am afraid not. But why must it be me? You say yourself that your daughter does not need a schoolmistress, that she reads and writes and does sums quickly. As for household management . . . "

He shook his head. "Nay, you still do not understand me. She will run the household well enough and have the servants in command; it is the airs and graces that she lacks. That is why I had hoped to find a young woman of society such as yourself to tutor her, you see, to put her in the way, as it were."

"Just how old *is* your daughter, Mr. Barstow?"

"Annie? Well, tha must let me figure. Annie will be . . ." He counted rapidly, moving the fingers on his hand in a quick curling motion. "Annie will be twenty-three come November." A shadow passed over his face. "My poor Maria bore her the end of the first year of our marriage, but she herself was gone before that Christmas. Yuletide has never been a happy time for me."

But he banished the mood abruptly. "However, we are not concerned with that at the moment, are we, miss? Will you meet with Annie? May I bring her to see you tomorrow?"

Briony gave him her hand. "Of course you may, Mr. Barstow; I shall look forward to it. Between now and then I shall try to come up with a substitute for myself whom you will find suitable."

"Aye. Well, as to that you know my feelings." He bowed over her hand in an awkward manner as if he were not much used to such courtly gestures. "We shall see you on the morrow, then?"

"Yes, why do you not come for luncheon? Most of the girls will have gone early in the day. Shall we say at two of the clock?"

His face creased in a broad grin, and she asked, "Why do you look surprised?"

"That be a bit late for my noonday meal, miss, but I expect Annie will take to it just fine."

3

"How VERY ODD, is it not, madame, that two such offers should come to you in two days? And so late in the season, too. Does it not make you think?"

"Make me think what, Mme. Vivienne?" asked Briony, looking up from the paperwork that would round off the ledger for the term.

The French mistress gave a Gallic shrug. "Mon Dieu, what can I say? Does it not seem suspiciously like the hand of Providence?"

Her employer chuckled. "I do not think, dear friend, that Providence is much concerned with cheating me out of my holiday. I should be very much annoyed with *le bon Dieu* if I thought such were the case."

Vivienne d'Artaud's hand flew to her mouth. "Oh, you must not make such a jest so! It ees a very foolish t'ing to do, *n'est-ce pas?*"

Briony put out a soothing hand. "Forgive me. I did not intend to make fun of the Deity, far from it. I believe that God has been extremely good to me these past few years, but do you not think *le bon Dieu* has a sense of humour since one was passed along to us?"

Vivienne d'Artaud sniffed. "If eet is so, madame, I 'ave never seen eet." Her own smile was ironic. "I do not mock, you understand. I merely accept what ees given to me, and I advise that you do the same, eh? One such visit of a rich man might be ignored, but two seem to be vairy suspicious."

"Suspicious?" Briony put down her quill. "In what way?"

But Madame d'Artaud merely pointed a secretive finger toward the ceiling as if to suggest that the Providence of whom she seemed to stand so much in awe was very poor of sight and would not pay attention to her doings if she kept silence.

Redmond, who had been sitting in the armchair reading *The Story of Rimini*, grimaced. "I say, how do you expect a chap to keep his concentration if you chatter like magpies?"

The French mistress sniffed. "I am regretful, monsieur, eef I disturb you. I did not evair know you to be so fascinated weeth a book before. Does it 'ave a great many pictures?"

The barb missed him completely. "I suppose not, but it is devilish romantic, you see. All about Paolo and Francesca and that Italian lot. An artist needs a bit of romance." His eyes half-closed dreamily. "I might even do a canvas on the subject. A large picture, I should think. It is an heroic episode after all."

When she giggled a little at that, he amended it. "Well, classic, in any case. On the other hand, one could conceive it in an almost miniature form because of the intimacy—a bright little jewel of a picture.

"What do you think, Bry? Big canvas or a miniature?"

His sister replied without even looking up, her voice abstracted and her manner inattentive. "I don't know, dear; not just now. I have totted up this column three times and reached three different sums." She put down the pen. "I wish I had Mr. Barstow's famous daughter to do them for me." She stopped and rubbed her eyes. "Perhaps I should stop and try again tomorrow."

"Let me just read you a bit of this, then," suggested Redmond eagerly, "since you are not going to work."

At such a threat Madame gathered up her embroidery materials and closed the sewing box with a snap. "I think per'aps I should finish my packing since I must leave so early."

"Oh, I say, I didn't offend you? I was only funning about the chatter, you know."

"Not at all, *m'sieu*, but I do not care for improper stories, and I believe that Francesca da Rimini was a vairy improper lady, indeed, is it not?"

At his stricken look, she patted his arm kindly. "As well as that, you see, I must 'ave my sleep of the beauty. Eet becomes more *difficile* each year to face the looking-glass, *hein*? Alas, one ees not young forevair.

"As for you, *ma cher* Briony, eef you are to interview the young woman of no consequence in the morning, you must not fill your head weeth figures. Add them up and let them go. Eef an error abides een there, the accountant weel discover eet, ees it not so?"

The headmistress pushed the ledger away from her. "I expect you are right." She lifted her cheek to be kissed by the older woman. "Sleep well, Vivienne."

"You as well, *ma petite*."

When the Frenchwoman had gone, Redmond ran a hand through his hair, tousling the Greek-curled locks. "Don't you think her odd, Bry?"

"Very odd and very dear," she agreed. "I don't know what I should have done without her as a sort of lieutenant these last few years. She is very fond of you as well, you know."

"As I am of her. But why does she call you madame every now and then, as if you were an old lady?"

"A mark of respect, I suppose. After all, I am her employer and the school's headmistress. I have certainly never asked it of her. Sometimes the girls use it as well; with them it is only a sort of affectation, but it sometimes makes me resent growing middle-aged before my time."

"I expect that is why you are so fixed upon this fling in Bath, is it not?"

"Exactly that. Never mind that I shall have to scrimp to do it, I truly need to get out of myself for a little while, even if it is only to be on the edge of things. Did you mean what you said about letting me go off by myself?"

Redmond shifted uncomfortably in his chair. "Would you mind awfully if I stayed away? I expect you won't need me. You will have beaux by the score the moment you arrive. You'll have to find some older lady to be your duenna."

"There is no more secure chaperone for a young woman than her own brother. Think it over again, Redmond, dear. Reconsider if you cannot postpone your visit to London for a little while."

Somewhat shamefacedly he promised. "Well, I will think about it, but, you see, I have rather promised this chap I know that I would share the rent of his studio. He is a good fellow; you remember I met him when he was on a painting excursion a month or two ago."

"But could you not paint in Bath Spa? I should think you would find subjects by the score."

"Not a bit of it. You must be joking. Far too much distraction for any serious work. I promise you that the temptation of the fleshpots would be mighty strong."

"I hardly think that Bath could be considered the equal of Sodom and Gomorrah, dear boy. You rather exaggerate."

"Still I had rather paint than play the social game."

Briony managed to smile tolerantly. "And you believe that a London artist's studio will be more monastic than a month or two in Bath? I fear your earnest hopes will be shattered; I hope you will not return a crushed man."

He chuckled as if he already suspected what temptations lay ahead and went off toward bed, perhaps to dream of them, but Briony remained, sitting over the ledgers and wondering if she had done the wise thing in rejecting the count's proposal out of hand; wondering as well what she would say to Mr. Barstow's daughter.

In the morning all was bustle, disorder, and farewells. All girls whose families had not already spirited them away were expected to be gone before midday. There was, of course, a great deal of anticipation of the holiday, but there were tears as well. Girls who had been bosom companions since arriving found it wrenching now to be torn apart. Occasionally a girl would even think to approach the headmistress's study. Señorita Ferreblanco from Havana could not contain her tears.

"I love my home, Miss Mitchem, and I am longing to see it again, but you have opened a whole new world to me. This English life is much different from ours in Cuba. And I have no one there, you know, but my papa. Even Tante Maria is dead."

"I am sure you will find you fit in again very quickly, Consuela."

"No, miss, I do not think I will. What shall I do without you to run to with my problems?"

"You must look forward to your new life, my dear. You have not seen your father in two years, and you are to be married at Christmastime!" Briony kissed her pupil reassuringly on the forehead. "You will be the first of this year's girls to be married, you know. By this time next year . . . well, who knows what joys you will be writing me about?"

"But I do not even know him. How can he make me happy?"

Briony looked at her sharply. She had heard of these arranged marriages, but she had never known one this extreme. "Do you mean to say you have never met him?"

Consuela shook her head violently. "Never. I have only seen his picture, the miniature that my papa sent me, and you know those painters lie. Don Pepe is a great man, I know, for he is the governor's friend, but to marry him without love? Oh, madame, why must I?"

Briony Mitchem was aware of those Spanish traditions in the Caribbean which mandated that daughters were merely chattel to be portioned out at best advantage, but, she also suspected, the girl had absorbed a great deal of the English way of looking at such things. Romantic novels were forbidden at the academy, but she could not help but be aware that they circulated surreptitiously among her charges. They had always seemed to her to be harmless until now.

She sat beside the girl on the settee and took Consuela's hand in her own. "My sweet little señorita, you knew this was what your father had planned. You were sent to England to educate you to take your place in your own society; I have even heard you boasting to the other girls what a great marriage had been made for you. Why are you suddenly so much against it?"

Consuela's face puckered, and she threw her head with a sob into Briony's lap. "Oh, Miss Mitchem, I am frightened! What if Don Pepe is a dreadful beast?"

Miss Mitchem, unfortunately, had no answer for that.

By noon the house was nearly empty. Vivienne d'Artaud had caught the ten o'clock post coach from Hadrian's Green amidst many embraces and protestations of affection.

"You are vairy sure, madame, that I should not come to ze Bath weeth you?"

"No, no, Vivienne, you have things to do in Paris, I am certain. I would not have you relinquish your holiday only to keep me company. Besides, I shall be living very quietly there; hardly anything to draw you away from the most fascinating city in the world."

"Fascinating? Paree? Oui, I suppose so," said the French mistress with a blasé shrug. "I should 'ave chosen London, instead, perhaps. Perhaps, even, you will one day visit Paree weeth me and let me see it t'rough new eyes, eh?"

By one o'clock, when she returned to the academy, it was deserted except for Mrs. Travers, the cook, and one little maidservant who would remain until Briony had left for Bath.

"It will be almost like a holiday beginning, Miss Briony, to make luncheon for only four," cook declared. "I wonder if I shall remember how to make less than twenty-five portions?" She shook her head, amused, "Them girls do make a difference."

But Briony, as she left the kitchen, saw a familiar dogcart coming along the drive. She immediately stepped back to speak to Mrs. Travers. "You had better increase the luncheon count to six, I think. I see Mr. Rawdon coming up the drive."

"Mr. Rawdon, is it?" asked cook with a heavenward look. "Then I had best plan for six. I know how he wolfs into the cucumber sandwiches. I am happy we have a fresh pot of mustard for him."

Briony smiled at the little jest, for it was a source of much neighbourhood amusement that the solicitor liked to spice up bland food with mustard and that it was applied to everything from chicken to potatoes.

Jonas Rawdon was a happy man, but no one looking at his long phiz and melancholy expression would have guessed it. He was one of those persons decreed by nature to function as gravediggers, nonconformist preachers, lawyers, or professional mourners, although within his heart there was a constant bubble of untainted joy. He had a fat, pretty wife and three jolly children who resembled him in not the slightest degree. He was, as well, blessed with an admirable digestion and the healthy appetite with which Mrs. Travers was acquainted. Briony met him at the top of the stairs leading up from the drive.

"The boy will come for your cart. I had not expected to see you again before I went on holiday."

He leapt to the ground gaily and wrapped the reins about the post. "That was why I hurried out here this afternoon. I have no idea when you are leaving for Bath nor have you furnished me with an address."

"I know I have not," she laughed. "Did you think it was an unintentional oversight? It was not. I want to be free for a little while. I want, just for a little, to forget Mitchem Academy and all of its affairs. I have balanced the books and closed the ledger and I want to think of nothing but the state of the weather and if the mineral water will improve my disposition."

He kissed her cheek fondly, for he had known her for a good many years, and, momentarily, his eyes were more serious than usual. "I am afraid you can never quite do that, my girl."

She read his face with care, then asked apprehensively, "I see that I must put off being carefree for another hour. It is trouble, isn't it? More debts?"

"We had best go inside," he suggested, and she led him into the library, where she poured him a sip of damson cordial from the crystal decanter that was one of the few treasures retained from the old regime of the house.

"I thought all of father's creditors had come forward."

He made a face at that. "So far as is certain they have done so. Naturally, more may surface, but I believe there is small likelihood of it."

A pang struck her heart. "Then these . . . not . . . ?"

He nodded sadly. "Yes, my child. I am afraid they are Redmond's."

"Artist's things, I expect? Material? Canvas and paints?"

"I wish it were so. The sum might be smaller if such were the case."

Briony bent her head and squeezed her eyes to shut out the facts she must face. "Gambling?"

"Yes."

So blood *did* tell? She had spent all these years scrimping and cutting corners, living on the lean side of the world, to pay off the mound of responsibilities her father had left behind, only to be faced with Redmond setting forth upon the same path?

"Are they bad?"

"Bad enough. Personally, I cannot imagine why anyone was foolish enough to allow him credit past a sixpence.

Everyone in the county knows the struggle you have had, how you have created this place from virtually nothing."

He showed her the figure and she paled. "What is your advice?"

He made a lawyer's gesture of disinvolvement. "To refuse them. Redmond is old enough now to stand for his own faults."

Her response was impatient. "I cannot simply abandon him to the hounds, Rawdon. The academy is as much his as mine. The very house belongs to him, as you well know." A thought struck terror in her. "Could they take the house?"

Rawdon looked grave, shook his head. "It is more valuable now than when your father died. It is unlikely that any judge in the county would approve such a claim, yet it is serious."

He rose and wandered about the room, examining the fine bindings of the many volumes without really seeing them individually. "These could be sold for a smart price, you know. Your father was God's great fool, but your grandsire laid in a fine book collection."

"No!" The abruptness of her rejoinder surprised even herself. "They took enough else. It was all I could do to hold on to the books and a little of the furniture. All the good things went: the Italian bed, the best of the paintings, the Grinling Gibbons' overpiece." She gazed defensively about the room. "All that is left are the books. These and Redmond are all I have left of the old days, and I will abandon none of them."

She thought sadly of the Graf von Ahlden and his offer. "You should have come to me a week ago; I might have had a solution."

But then, then she remembered the handsome ironmaster, and she clapped her hands.

"Rawdon, I hope you are free to stay for nuncheon?"

"I shall be gratified, but what . . . ?"

"Wait, just wait! You shall see!"

— 4 —

PRECISELY AT TWO o'clock the brougham bearing the iron-master and his daughter came up the drive and stopped before the south front. The coachman on the box was smartly attired in yellow and green, a white cockade jauntily adorning his tricorne. The lad beside him, similarly garbed but cockadeless, leapt down and opened the carriage door with a cheeky grin.

" 'Ere we are, sir. Looks quite grand, dunnit?"

Barstow, descending, gave him an affectionate cuff. "You must learn to mind your manners, boy. This be a civilized part of the world, not a sink-hole like that Lunndon of yours nor full up with earth-moles like mine."

The lad understood that, though the words were jocular, the intention of them was serious and meant to be taken to heart. He touched a finger to forehead in salute. "Right you are, sir. I'll remember, sir!"

Barstow beamed on him. "There's a good lad. Model yourself on Joseph up there on t'box and you will not go far wrong." Joseph-the-coachman merely sniffed, affecting not to hear. Only hard times had thrown him into the employ of this upstart ironmaster. Still, it was true what the man said. And the lad had shown himself bright and eager enough to learn.

Their employer turned back to the carriage and held his arm for the young woman to descend. Her travelling-veil obscured her face, but her figure was fashionably slim and well-formed.

The costume she had chosen, however, was dreadful.

It was clear that it had originally had been conceived as an honest kerseymere pelisse, but the tailoring, in the first place, was poor, and to disguise the deficiencies of the cut a great deal of ill-advised trimming had been added: velvet braid, epaulettes and cuffs of thick purple velvet. With it she wore a truly undistinguished bonnet of levantine. The effect was altogether both cheap and showy, quite unsuited to the natural elegance of the young woman's movement and carriage. But as she ascended the steps to the house, Anne Barstow threw back the travelling veil which had protected her face from the dust of the road and revealed a countenance that was almost perfect in its symmetry. The shape of her face was oval, her mouth full but not extraordinarily wide, and her nose quite classic in shape and proportion. It was her eyes, however, which invariably held the attention of any spectator: large and calm and of an extraordinary depth which gave beauty rather than forcing her to suffer from a mere prettiness. Briony was quite taken aback when this goddess thrust out her hand and, in a tone of astonishing ugliness, cawed, "Tha knows my da has praised 'ee to the skies, I expect, miss."

Briony could feel Jonas Rawdon, beside her, stiffen as if his sense of fitness had been deliberately outraged, that this ill-garbed goddess should have a tongue of clay.

Introductions were made all round, and the Barstows were led into the drawing room. "Nuncheon will be served presently," Briony explained. "May I offer you gentlemen a cordial? And you, Miss Barstow?"

Anne Barstow did not so much look abashed as pained and sorrowful that such a suggestion should even have been made to her. "I am a chapel-goer, Miss Mitchem. I have never allowed spirits to pass my lips."

"Tha mayest give her barley water if tha has some by," her father suggested, "but a drop of cordial will do me very well."

Briony first tugged the bell-cord and then poured the

damson. Rawdon rolled his about on his tongue as if he had not had opportunity to appreciate his first glass, but Barstow tossed his back and held out his goblet for a refill.

"A bit more this time would do no hurt," he commented. "It has a pleasant flavour."

When the little maidservant appeared and was asked if there were any barley water in the kitchen, she seemed taken aback. "I don't know as we have made up any, miss, since Rachel were taken sick at St. Agnes's Day Fair."

"Oh, I do not wish to give trouble," Anne protested. "A glass of water will do me well enough to wet my weasand. The drive were terribly dusty."

The maidservant's eyes went rather round as she gazed upon the speaker, but she made her bob, then hurried belowstairs. "I don't know what is coming about," she said to cook, "when Miss Briony is entertaining common people of that sort in the drawing room. My word, and got up like a fairground!"

Mrs. Travers shook her finger. "Never you mind. If Miss Briony has them in the drawing room, they be gentry, even if they talks odd." She drew forth an earthenware jug from the back of the pantry, shook it, then poured forth its fluid into a glass. Placing it upon a tray with a napkin beside it, she handed it to the girl to carry upstairs.

"You remember, now, what I said. And just mention to Miss Briony on the quiet that nuncheon will be a quarter of an hour late."

The quartet chose to spend the time in strolling about the near edges of the park; Rawdon and the ironmaster with seegars, discussing the state of business, the British ascension over the Rajput states and Poona, as well as the distressing refusal of Parliament to recognize the nation's imminent peril from French imports.

"For I tell you, Rawdon, t' English can get as drunk as David's sow on our own gin without the Frenchies adding their beverages," Barstow said.

Rawdon regarded him with quiet amusement. "I rather

thought from your daughter's words that you were close to abstention in your part of the world."

The muscular ironmaster guffawed. "You heard me ask for more of the cordial?" He licked his lips. "That had a bit of kick for coming from a lady's decanter, you know."

The ladies strolled along the stream bank, Briony admiring once again her guest's Grecian profile. Anne, as if feeling Miss Mitchem's eyes, blushed and ventured to say diffidently, "I daresay we are being a bother, but Da *would* have it that I should meet you." She smiled. "He is that taken with his 'grand Miss Mitchem.' "

"I am very gratified," said Briony. "Your father is a most persuasive man with an enormous charm."

"Yes," Anne agreed. "All the widows pursue him, and he has quite given up going to chapel because of it."

Briony was not sure whether this was an example of a sly northern humour or straight-faced reportage, so she did not take it up. She could well imagine, however, that in his own part of the world the still youngish ironmaster might well be considered a prime catch.

"And you, Miss Barstow, what do you want out of life?"

She was astonished at the vehemence with which the reply came. "I want to eat it up, miss. The life up there in the border country is all very well, tha understands; they are good people, kind and honest people, but"— she spread her hands wide in despair—"but it is such a big world and there are so many things to do and to see! I want to have my own look at it, Miss Mitchem. Not out of books, tha kens, but out of my own two eyes."

Here was a spirit that Briony had not suspected from the young woman's prim refusal of the cordial. She could understand, all too well, the drive that made the ironmaster's daughter wish to improve herself and widen her horizons.

Now from the direction of the house she could see the little maidservant coming across the sward. "Yes, Polly, what is it?"

"Two more for nuncheon, miss. The gentleman was here before, he says. I have put them in the library, if that is all right, miss?"

"Perfectly right, Polly." She turned back to Anne Barstow, but the girl waved her away.

"Tha had best go quickly. I can join the gentlemen or look at your lovely garden."

"Can I depend on you to herd the gentlemen toward the house presently?"

Anne beamed at the easy acceptance she was shown. "Oh, aye. In t' north we learn early how men must be managed."

It was, as she had somehow suspected, the Graf von Ahlden, but she found him not in the library but the drawing room, and not accompanied but alone.

"Good afternoon, sir. I am surprised to see you again."

He took it calmly. "I told you I would return, though I fear, I met with a short delay and had to return to my own country on urgent business."

He sat down again, leaning his cane against the arm of his chair, and rubbed his hands like a shopkeeper. "Now then, are you ready to resume?"

"Resume, your lordship?" Briony asked. "I had believed my answer was already given."

He nodded sagely. "Umm, yes. But I thought that perhaps, after consideration, you might have come to a different opinion."

Despite her new need for money, something about his manner annoyed her to the point of answering, "No, I have not."

"Then nothing has changed?" he asked with raised eyebrows.

He was getting at something, she sensed, but she must wait to know what it was. "No, nothing. Why do you ask?"

He leaned back in the French fauteuil, regarding her with an infuriating curl of the lips that almost, though not quite, settled into a smirk. "We all meet with unexpected reverses from time to time, Miss Mitchem. I suspect that your financial margins are very narrow, and I merely wanted to be certain you had not changed your mind. It *is* a substantial amount of money I am offering, you know. I daresay it illustrates my confidence in your abilities. I expect it was in my mind that you would eventually see your way to cooperation with me in this venture."

From a distance she heard the front entrance door bang, then Redmond's voice call out her name. "Bry! Bry! Are those people gone?"

Some premonitory warning flashed through Briony's mind just as Redmond paused in the doorway of the drawing room. "Bry, have you . . . ?"

Then he caught sight of von Ahlden. "Oh," he said stiffly, "I had not realised you were not alone." He took a deep breath, and she saw that his face had gone very white, the muscles of his jaw tense and his nostrils flared. He spoke directly to the count.

"There was no reason, sir, for you to trouble my sister. You had my word as a gentleman that my debt to you would be honoured."

His lordship acknowledged this with a slight inclination of his head. "So you did, young sir, and I agreed to wait for a short time. That being the case, have you considered that Miss Mitchem and I might be discussing something quite unrelated to *our* previous encounter?"

"What encounter?" asked Briony suspiciously.

Then she knew.

"Oh, Redmond, what have you blundered into this time?"

The youth flushed madly. "Well, I say, Bry, it isn't altogether my fault. This man . . . "

Briony stopped him with an upraised hand. "I gather you have not been introduced? Your lordship, may I present my brother, Redmond Mitchem? Redmond, his lordship, the Graf von Ahlden."

The count smiled coolly. "I expect that at our previous

meeting your brother was not aware that I had already had the pleasure of your acquaintance."

"And you," she said accusingly, recalling the details Rawdon had given her, "were the man at the Blue Boar who played against my brother when anyone else would have shied away like a skittered horse?"

"An admirable simile, dear lady, quite military." He tapped the point of his cane lightly against the floor for emphasis as he went on. "Do please, Fräulein Mitchem, consider my position. I have a major task to perform within a little more than two months. I certainly cannot hope to accomplish it alone, and so I must enlist"—he struggled for a simile—" 'aiders and abetters,' would you say in English?"

"I believe the correct word might be 'accomplices,' your lordship." But his expression was at once so guileless and so sly that Briony could not help smiling a little. "Your methods are somewhat less than laudable, sir."

"Time is of the essence. Are we agreed?"

She saw her holiday slipping inexorably away. "Very well. I know when I am beaten."

"What is going on here?" Redmond demanded impatiently. "I feel as if I have come late to a playhouse."

"I believe," said his lordship, "that your sister and I have just completed an agreement where she will undertake a special task for two months of her holiday."

"What? Give up your famous trip to Bath? Oh, Briony, I feel wretched that you are not going to have your . . ." His eyes narrowed. "Wait a moment. Are you saying that I was lured into gambling with this man . . . and that I was cheated?"

"I think you should understand, young sir, that 'cheat' is not a word that gentlemen bandy about in jest. As I recall, after the first hand of cards I tried to withdraw. Is that not so? Do you not remember how you all but begged me to continue?"

"Is that true, Redmond?" asked his sister.

He shuffled his feet, still an adolescent in many respects. "I . . . yes, I expect so."

"You *expect* so?"

"Well, then, yes. It is true." He hunched his shoulders and looked miserable. "I suppose I am just a deuced bad player."

"Oh good," she said enthusiastically, "then I shall not be alone in this venture."

"What do you mean?" he asked in alarm.

"If I go, my dear boy, you go. This is to pay off your debts, not mine! And you will work for it, I do assure you."

"But my plans for London . . . I have agreed to share a studio!"

His sister merely looked at him with a level gaze that made him drop his own eyes in shame. "Very well," he said. "I expect the fool must pay the piper."

"But," Briony said to von Ahlden, "this is all contingent upon the young woman. When will she arrive in England? When can I have the pleasure of meeting her?"

"As to that," the count said, "it is easily enough remedied. I have left her to browse through your magnificent library."

Polly tapped lightly at the door of the drawing room. "If you please, miss, luncheon will be served in five minutes."

"Thank you, Polly. Count, you and your ward will join us, of course? Redmond, be kind enough to summon Mr. Rawdon and the Barstows from the garden." She paused, counting in her head. "My word, we shall have a full table, shall we not?"

Redmond disappeared gratefully through the long window into the garden, and Briony threw open the double doors to the book room.

= 5 =

THE LIBRARY OF Mitchem House was lavish in the old fashion; architecturally elegant proportions with the furnishings having been designed by the same hand. It was a paradise of fine binding, rich in the scent of leather and comfort. It had been her father's favourite retreat when exhausted by the tables, and it was Briony's private retreat from the girls.

The young woman who sullenly faced them as they entered was as out of place amidst this handsomeness as a toad in a bridal-bower. There was no doubt but that she was profoundly unattractive: overweight by some thirty-five pounds, hair which hung in greasy strands, and a spotty complexion caused, Briony guessed, as much from improper eating as from careless cleansing. Clutched in the young woman's pudgy hand was a cloisonné comfit box which the headmistress knew had been filled only this morning.

She put the box down with an arrogant scowl. "Well, von Ahlden, have you succeeded in your mission? No, I can see from your face that you have failed once again. I knew it was a hopeless case. May we go home again now, or must we prolong the embarrassment I am certain we all feel?"

"Your highness," said the count, "may I have the honour of presenting Miss Briony Mitchem, headmistress of Mitchem Academy?

"Miss Mitchem, Her Highness the Princess Isabella Wittelsbach of Schleswig-Holstein-Gundorp-Thoningen."

Briony swept into a deep curtsey. "Your highness, welcome to my home."

"Home? I thought this was a school? Von Ahlden, you told me this was a school." Her English was clear with only the slightest in foreign intonation, but her manner was petulant and abrasive. Briony was particularly struck by the timbre of her voice, rich as velvet, despite the brusqueness.

"It was my home long before it was a school, your highness."

Isabella made a wide gesture. "And these books? I expect you inherited them all and have read very few?"

"When I was a girl," Briony answered, "I vowed that I would someday read every volume in this room, and I have made considerable progress. I have a long way to go, but I trust I will have many years in which to do it."

The princess relented just a trifle. "It is a superb collection, both beautiful and comprehensive. I could lose myself here for hours."

Von Ahlden seemed to regard this as a trap. "Too much of a temptation just now, your highness. Even if Miss Mitchem should accept you, you would not be studying here."

"Really?" asked Briony. "Whyever not?"

"For reasons of the princess's safety; your park encroaches rather too closely upon the lawn for my peace of mind. In any case, Miss Mitchem, I believe you are correct in believing you need a change of scene. The work you will be doing with her highness will be both intensive and time-consuming. It is my belief that, for best results, it should also be a pleasure. I have a fear that forcing you to remain here when you are so eager to get away would turn the task into drudgery and ultimately defeat our purpose."

"Which is?"

The princess stepped forward into the light and gestured at herself in a despairing way. "Look at me and you will see. I am a fat German cow, *nein*? I expected to be a spinster aunt locked away in a library, spending my days with bon bons and pet cats." Her eyes sparkled with sudden tears. "And yet they have told me I am to marry in the autumn. It is all arranged; a matter of political convenience, you say, and no love expected or lost, is it not so? But there is a man involved who is to share my bed and look at me across the table. A very handsome man! I cannot ask him to accept me like this." Her face crumpled. "He would hate me forever."

"But why have you . . . ?" Briony impulsively began to ask, then checked herself. But the princess divined her meaning.

"Why have I allowed myself to wait so long? I could not truly believe such a marriage contract would ever be completed. To marry Rudolph is the shock of my life."

"Rudolph? You cannot mean Duke Rudolph?"

"You see?" the princess asked. "Even you are astonished. Think, then, how it affected me to be told I was to marry Duke Rudolph of Berengaria."

Briony was amazed, for the handsome Duke Randolph was, at this moment in history, rightly considered the prime matrimonial catch of Europe. During Napoleon's ascendancy the throne of the hereditary duchy to which he was heir had almost fallen prey to the emperor's scheme of mediatization, which would have left Rudolph's father with his title but very little real authority as his duchy was absorbed into the larger state. After Waterloo, however, the Treaty of Vienna had resettled the boundaries of Europe, to some extent restoring the legitimate dynasties. Now, as a premier member of the German Confedertaion, Berengaria and its new ruler were at the peak of the royal marriage list. International gossip had suggested many possible brides for the young duke, but never had Briony heard it said that Isabella Wittelsbach was among them.

The princess seemed in despair, all aloofness and truculence gone. "If Rudolph should despise me, it would be the marriage of your Prince Regent to my cousin Caroline all over again and a marriage of no use to anyone."

Briony's heart went out to her, but it was not until she herself turned to von Ahlden with a question about the financial arrangements that she realized that she had all unconsciously already made the decision. It was difficult to bargain before Isabella, but she forced herself to do it.

"Very well," she said at length. "My brother's debt to you will be forgiven, all expenses of the experiment are to be borne by you, and a paid holiday in Bath Spa for myself when we are done."

She could not miss the look of triumphal complicity which passed between the count and his ward. She suspected she could have asked for a great deal more and received it.

"Agreed," the count said. "Now we must go to our luncheon, yes?"

"Not quite," said Briony. "There are other considerations which must be met before a final agreement."

He did not appear surprised, but, perhaps, a little wary. "Ah? And what considerations might they be?"

The headmistress put her fingers before her in a steeple fashion as she considered. "It seems to me quite obvious that I cannot accomplish very much in such a short time without assistance and complete cooperation. Is that understood?"

"Oh, completely."

"I must have a free hand to employ whatever helpers I see fit and to employ them in any way I choose?"

"Certainly. You will be in charge, fräulein."

"And you, your highness, do you agree? Am I to completely be your governess for these two months? Your mentor in everything?"

"In everything, Miss Mitchem," said Isabella with suspicious docility. Briony wondered how difficult it would be for the young woman to temporarily lay aside the sense of rank which had been inborn into her.

"Also, I believe your highness will do better if you feel you do not have to face this task alone. I do not wish you to set up barriers to your progress because you have grown to hate me."

"Please? To hate you?" Briony again marvelled at the beauty of that darkly coloured voice. "How could I hate someone who is to be my saviour?"

"It is a hazard teachers often face, madame. The pupil who resents authority sometimes turns against the very one who is trying to help her. In order to diffuse this resentment I would like to suggest the addition of still another person to the program."

"Very well thought out," said von Ahlden. "An assistant, yes?"

"No," said Briony, "another pupil.".

He frowned. "Oh, but I do not know if this is possible or wise." Isabella made no response. "Who is this second person?"

"You will meet her at luncheon," Briony promised. "You will find her acceptable, I believe; but without her I do not wish to go further. She and the princess will help each other in many ways, I think. They are so unalike that this cannot help but be so."

Von Ahlden did not agree, but he offered no further resistance to the idea. "There is something else?" asked Isabella.

"It may be difficult for you, your highness."

"Ah? What is it that is so difficult, Miss Mitchem?"

"During your stay in England you must remain incognito."

"*That* is a provision? It is a matter of course!"

Briony shook her head firmly. "I mean completely so, Isabella. While under my direction you will have no rank, no consideration more than another, and there would be absolutely no mention of your background or your family or your marriage. You would be a cypher, a person of no particular importance. I think it would be wise to decide upon your incognito now, before nuncheon, and hold to it for the length of your stay."

Isabella clapped together her pudgy hands. "Oh, what fun. What a fine idea. I shall have no responsibilities if I take on a new person, eh? I love the provision, not hate it."

"I am not sure of this," von Ahlden protested. "A certain respect must certainly be retained."

"No," Briony said, "that is my point. No respect whatsoever is due a nameless pupil save that inherent in herself. Her highness would be no longer a princess, only a young woman who would be expected to work very, very hard in order to transform herself."

"Oh, *ja wohl*, to be nobody! Wunderbar!"

"And," Briony concluded, "it must be agreed from the first that the cancellation of Redmond's debt is contingent upon nothing. I make no promises except that I will do my utmost. The progress of the princess . . ."

"Isabella," said her new pupil. "I am a princess no longer. I am only Isabella."

"The progress of Isabella will depend entirely upon herself. It will be difficult, you know. You will hate the work if you do not hate me."

"But why must she share your attention?" von Ahlden asked.

"Because I believe that she and her companion will have much to teach each other, as I have said. You shall judge for yourself. Shall we join the others?"

"Yes," the count said. "Let me meet them and decide. I am not happy about it. Her highness—Isabella, that is—will require personal attention. I do not see how you can divide your focus between them."

"I do not intend to do so," Briony said. "I think, as well, that you should be warned that her father is a determined and plain-spoken man. I have made no mention of my plan to him, and he may, in fact, not approve of *you*."

"Well, then," said Isabella imperiously, "let us see who this person may be." She strode purposefully toward the door.

"Isabella," Briony cautioned, "we may as well begin now. In English society there are certain rules of precedence. We follow them here as well."

"Yes? Well? I am ready to follow them."

"I think . . . Isabella . . . ," said the count, "that Miss Mitchem is saying that in the groves of academe, the tutor precedes the pupil."

The Princess of Schleswig-Holstein-Gundorp-Thoningen looked annoyed, then her tension fell away as she relaxed.

"Of course," she said. "Where are my manners?"

= 6 =

THE LUNCHEON HAD been an odd one, Briony reflected when late in the day she was at last alone. Each pair of the quartet of guests had shown a lively interest in the other, while the fifth, Rawdon, had leant into the victuals with gusto, though still managing to keep his attention on the others.

Redmond, too, had been attentive. It was obvious that he found Miss Barstow more than attractive, despite the fact that he winced whenever she opened her mouth. Isabella had eaten with eyes cast down as if she were uncomfortable in company. It seemed to Briony that Isabella's guardian, the count, also cast many glances in Miss Barstow's direction, while the ironmaster seemed much interested in the state of industry in the German Confederation since the end of the war.

"You must tell me, your lordship, if you will, is there an increase of the mining in Thoningen? I understand that a high ore content comes out of your mountains, eh?" And the count, a most amiable man, indulged the father while looking covertly at the daughter, though it was most evident that he had little interest in the topic at hand.

Polly, the little maidservant, proved herself in the matter of service. She had scurried up and down, back and forth, with a willing air, presenting dishes, removing plates and replenishing glasses. Briony made a mental note to reward both Polly and cook, who had outdone herself in the crunch, with soup and sandwiches, a lovely bit of game pie topped off with trifle. Barstow had shown his appreciation by rivalling Rawdon, and even the count had asked for a bit more of the conserve.

It was just as the afternoon was drawing to an end that the ironmaster drew Briony aside for a private word.

"I wonder, miss, if you have given any further thought to the matter we discussed yesterday? You have seen my Anne, now, and you must have some notion?"

"As it happens I have given your situation some thought, sir. Have you time to step into my study for a few moments?"

"Aye, with pleasure. Let me just see what the girl is about if tha pleases."

But Anne was well settled with Redmond on one side and the count on the other, strolling about the lawn, while Rawdon trailed behind, munching on a golden pear, the juice running unchecked down his chin. As she turned away from the window Briony glanced through the door of the study and saw Isabella slipping unobtrusively back into the library. *That*, she thought, *is something which must be changed*.

The first thing Barstow said as he settled into his chair was direct and to the point. "You have decided to go with the count and the stout lass, eh? That is why you said no to me."

He had a sorrowful look about him as he said it. "You might have saved me the trip, lass. 'Twould have been kind."

There was something about this sturdy, forthright man that Briony liked immensely, but she had no intention of allowing personal feeling to interfere with business. "He is paying a great deal of money, Mr. Barstow, which I need to settle a debt."

"Well, miss, if it is only money that is wanted . . ."

She held up a hand to stop him. "It is a debt of honour about which I knew nothing when we spoke yesterday. I was being quite straightforward with you at that time."

"But now things have changed?" He narrowed his eyes, calculating. "Are you in the game for a bargain, miss? If you should take my Anne instead of that great lump of a girl, I will pay half again what the count will give 'ee."

"No," Briony assured him, "that is not the point."

"Money is always a point, I've found, miss. Double, then."

She had to laugh because he would not allow her to explain. "Will you wait a moment, sir?"

He laughed as well, good-humouredly believing he could overwhelm her. "Twice over and a half."

It was getting out of hand. She brought her palm down flat on the desk with a slapping sound. "Mr. Barstow, please."

"I shall have no respect for you, miss, if you are fool enough to turn down such an offer. I suppose it is because the count has a title, and I am only a rich upstart from the north, but my Annie shows more promise in her little finger than that great girl does in all . . ."

"Mr. Barstow," she said quietly, and he immediately ceased his tirade, blushing furiously.

Ducking his head, he said, "I daresay I do get carried away at times, but my Annie . . ."

"Your Annie is a very beautiful young woman with much natural grace and enormous charm, but she has, I fear, one or two major flaws which will hinder her from achieving the place she deserves."

"Did *I* not say that to you?" he asked in exasperation. "Why have you the face to tell back to me the very things I have been saying?"

Briony all but rolled her eyes. "You believe that, sir, because you will not hear me out. If you will let me have a word, I believe you will understand."

"I believe you have had many a word. Too many, I daresay!" He rose from his chair, visibly restraining his anger from explosion.

But Briony, too, was annoyed. "You are a great man in

your part of the world, I have no doubt," she began "but . . ."

"So now you are going to explain to me my own faults as well as my daughter's? You are a chit, miss."

"And you, sir, are a great booby!" The headmistress's voice rose unconsciously.

"And you . . . you are . . . " and he stopped, stricken at his rank discourtesy. An expression of chagrin came over his face, and his shoulders slumped.

"A booby, am I? Aye, I daresay. A great booby and a fool. Well, I have made my best offer, Miss Mitchem, and you have refused it, and we are done, I expect." He put out his hand. "No bad feeling, I hope?"

"No, Mr. Barstow," she said, "I have *not* refused your very generous offer." She smiled at him. "As you would have found if you had allowed me to say so."

It was wonderful to see the way these few words could light up a man's face.

"Do you mean to say you'll take her on?" He sat down heavily. "Woosh! You gave me a great fright."

"I will 'take her on,' as you say, only on certain conditions," Briony answered.

"Ah, so there are conditions?" he asked warily.

"No, wait. I have a plan, you see. I wish to take on *both* girls together. I believe that each will help the other."

This surprised him as much as anything she had said. "What, my Annie can help that high-nosed lump? You are serious? Well, if you say she may, I will believe it, though I cannot see how."

Briony had a deep affection for her brother, but she did not mean to let him get round her this time. "I cannot think how you were such a fool as to be duped into play so far above your head. You could not help but lose."

He grinned engagingly and sipped the posset cook had made them against the cool of the evening. "Ah, but what if the cards had gone with me and I had won? Just think what plans you would have had for the money."

"Pray do not bandy words with me, sir. If you had won

you would have been off to London like a shot from a pistol and you know it." He looked as if he would protest, but she stared him down until he flinched. "But the fact remains that you did *not* win, and I am, as usual, left to bail you out."

"Oh, come now. That was a scheme of the count's to snag you, Bry, and you know it. He would never try to collect. The very idea is absurd."

The laughter left Briony's eyes. "Would you not have taken his money if the game had gone in your direction?"

"Of course, I am not an idiot."

"Then you must help me pay him." She leaned foward across the chess table, dislodging the queen. "It is a debt of honour, Redmond, It is time you grow up. You cannot play the fool any longer. You have a responsibility to me, if to none other.

"Unless," she added quietly, "that means nothing to you."

Redmond hung his head. "You make me out to be a desperate rake."

She had to smile. "You seem to have set your feet in that direction." Then she was serious again. "Don't you understand, Redmond, that we must erase the stain father left behind. The world must know that the Mitchems are not a family to be dismissed with contempt."

"Why does it mean so much to you? I daresay you will marry soon and have another name altogether.

"But I understand what you are saying to me, and I will do as you ask."

Her face brightened. "I knew you would. I never believed for a moment that you would let me down."

He was silent for a few minutes, idly moving the chess pieces this way and that. "The thing is, Bry,"—he looked as if he were experiencing a bad taste in his mouth—"that the ironmaster's daughter is fine enough in looks, so long as she keeps silent, but that Fräulein Wittelsbach is rather a pill, isn't she?"

"All the more reason she will need special attention from

the start." He made a face. "It is only for two months, Redmond. It cannot be so bad as all that."

"I will try for your sake, Briony. Only because I love you."

"For your own sake, sir, as well," she said ironically, "unless you have a jingle in your pocket that I know nothing of."

Upon examination of the house the Graf von Ahlden had selected, Miss Mitchem pronounced herself suited well enough, there being ample room for herself, staff, and pupils—her own staff only, of course, for the servants were hired with the house. She had yet, however, to *find* her assistants. One in particular she felt was necessary, but difficult to come by. She needed someone trained in particular fashion to overcome the deficiencies each young woman exhibited.

With this in mind she boarded the post coach, and, with Redmond at her side and little Polly in tow, she set out for London.

It was the second week of June, and, though the country-side was in its glory, London was in its prime. As they jounced through the streets Redmond pointed out first this sight and then that: churches, parks, coffeehouses. Neither Briony nor Polly had ever seen such elegance as was visible in the handsome new buildings, the fashionable men and women who promenaded through St. James's Park, the elegant shops whose windows were crowded with the most exquisite of merchandise. It was a very great trial not to yield to the ever-present temptation of spending some of her money on herself, rather than business, but she held fast. The count had placed all authority in her hands, leaving her to go about her business as she saw fit. He would never know what expenditures were made, but it was for this very reason that Briony must cleave to the straight and narrow. Such trust as that should not be broken.

She sent a message off by the innkeeper's boy within an hour of their arrival and within another hour had received a reply. If she would be kind enough to present herself at the offices of Mr. Jarndyce the following morning at ten, it might be that something could be done on her behalf.

That evening she allowed Redmond to lure her off to the theatre, where they saw a charmingly old-fashioned play, *The Man of Mode*, which was full of wicked rakes and women of no account. She understood, of course, from the rowdy laughter which greeted many of the lines, that there were jokes and epigrams which passed completely over her head. Even Redmond seemed remarkably worldly in this respect, but, she reckoned, it was because he was a man and more privy to certain mysteries than she. Over a late supper in a nearby chophouse, they discussed their particular errands in town.

"I hope you will not mind, Bry, if I desert you tomorrow. I must find this chap, you know, who promised me the use of his studio to explain why I cannot spend the summer. Though how I shall break it to him, I am sure I do not know."

"The simplest way would be to say the unvarnished truth, I should think," his sister advised. "There is no shame in honouring an obligation."

"There is a bit of shame in having to say I have been such a dupe at cards," Redmond retorted. "But I expect there is no other way."

From across the room a florid gentleman seemed to be trying to catch Briony's eye. He nodded and smiled and tipped his hat, but Redmond scowled so fiercely at him and Briony looked so blank that he soon gave up his efforts. However, as he left the dining room, he spoke into the ear of his waiter, inclining his head toward the Mitchems. The waiter smiled and nodded respectfully and, when the gentleman had gone, approached their table. He was a tall thin man with a sonorous voice.

"Mr. Jarndyce would like you to take a glass of wine and

a dessert at his expense," he said respectfully. "I beg your pardon, but are you an actress, miss?"

"An actress? Good heavens, no."

"Are you being impertinent?" asked her brother.

The waiter hastened to deny it. "Not at all, sir. Far from it. But the lady being so handsome and her knowing Mr. Jarndyce and being *here* and all. Well, I naturally wondered, you see. We don't have much but theatre folk, you see, in this particular inn. Mr. J. says he quite looks forward to tomorrow."

"Who the devil is Mr. Jarndyce?" Redmond demanded. Briony broke into merry laughter, then put her hand to her mouth to stifle it.

"Oh, my very dear! That was the gentleman with whom I have an appointment tomorrow morning. The father of one of my old pupils. And I did not recognize him! That is why he was sending me those peculiar looks and winks. My, and I thought I was in danger of being abducted!"

"Not from the Seven Dial Chophouse, I should hope, miss!" said the waiter indignantly in his rich Shakespearean voice. "We may be theatrical, but we are quite respectable!"

"And not while I am with you, I hope," said her brother with equal indignation. "Good Lord, Bry, what do you think of me?"

"I am sure you are very dear and very gallant," she pronounced. "And I also think that for this dessert I will have a glass of port wine and a plum tart."

"A very fine selection, miss, if you allow me to say so," congratulated the waiter. "The plum is particularly fine here. Quite famous, actually."

"Then," said Redmond, "as I am included, I shall have the same."

=== 7 ===

MR. JARNDYCE HAD his offices in a building adjoining that theatre in Oxford Street which bore his name. Miss Mitchem and her maidservant were shown directly into his private sanctorum by an obsequious clerk who all but scraped the floor with his bowing. The manager immediately arose from his desk and came forward, hands outstretched, to meet them.

"My dear Miss Mitchem, it has been too long. I trust I did not disconcert you in the Dials last evening. I was not certain you recognised me and so I chose not to intrude upon you and your handsome young man."

"My brother," she murmured.

"Ah, your brother?" His tone grew warmer. "How long has it been since we met? Two years, is it? I don't wonder that you had forgotten my face."

"I shall not soon forget the dessert you so kindly provided, Mr. Jarndyce. It was quite delicious. The plum tart."

"For which they are justly famous," he acknowledged. "Ah, well and good. And the waiter? What did you think of him?"

Briony racked her brain. "He had a very beautiful voice," she answered. "That is all that I recall."

"Exactly," he said enigmatically. "Exactly."

Now he stepped back from her, surveying her trim and tailored travelling costume. "How efficient you look! Quite like a woman of authority should do. Is this what school-mistresses wear up to town?"

She could not say if he were serious or speaking in jest, but she blushed and answered that she believed so. Certainly she had chosen this round style dress in that belief.

Jarndyce nodded. "Yes, yes, I am sure." He went to the door of his office and snapped his fingers imperiously. The clerk who had escorted them in now bounced into the room, striking an attitude of expectation.

"Take note of what Miss Mitchem is wearing, Walsingham," said the manager. "Draw a little sketch if you feel it necessary. This is what a respectable schoolmistress wears up to town from the country. I believe it is just what we want for Act Three."

Walsingham agreed at once. "Exactly what is needed, sir! Do you mind turning just a trifle, Miss Mitchem?

"And the girl, sir? For the maid's costume?"

"No, no, you fool, quite wrong. Anyone can see that."

"Oh, yes. Quite, sir. What could I have been thinking of?" He scribbled several lines on a bit of paper. "And the material, sir?"

Jarndyce turned to Briony. "I expect you think we are mad, but I like to have things in my plays quite right, you see. Especially the modern ones."

"The material is ordinary Wilton stuff," Briony said. "You should have no trouble finding it."

"Very kind of you, I am sure. Well, Walsingham? Out. Out. You have no more business here, man. Get to it."

He smiled again at Briony. "I hope I find you well?"

"Oh, very well. And you, sir? I know you are prospering, for your daughter Celia writes me often. She tells me that your theatre is enjoying an enormous success. What is the play called? Is it *The Frozen Deep*?"

"Exactly that. I hope that you and your brother—and even your little friend here"—he twinkled at Polly—"will be my guests at the theatre tonight. Unless you have previous plans? Do you know London well?"

"No," Briony answered, "I do not. This is the first visit I have made since my parents died several years ago. Even then, I was merely an occasional visitor."

"Then you must let me show you about. My pleasure.

"London is my town," he said expansively. "There is everything here, you know, everything a man could wish for. Why, as old Johnson used to say, 'The man who has grown tired of London has grown tired of life.' Or at least, so my father used to quote him. My father was seldom wrong about such things. Drove my mother half mad with them, quoting all the time. Where are you putting up?"

"At the Bell Savage in Ludgate."

He seemed to approve. "Not grand, but respectable, I believe, and clean."

Briony agreed. "Although it was the only name I knew. It is the coach terminus, you see. I am sure we shall all be happy to visit the theatre, Mr. Jarndyce, although I regret to say we shall be leaving again in a day or two."

"What a pity. I find London just a bit lonely, you know, since Celia married and went off to Falmouth," he confided.

"And your wife, sir?"

His face grew sad. "Celia's stepmother ran off with a tenor eighteen months ago. I expect she found him more entertaining than an old stick like myself. She was playing comedy in the north, the last I heard of her. The man's been back for some time, so I expect she has found another haven.

"A fine, fine actress, you know," he added generously. "I daresay she will tire of the road and come back to London one of these days." He slapped his thigh and sprang to his feet in a sudden change of mood. "However, we had best get on with the purpose of your visit, eh?"

"I will appreciate any suggestions you may have."

"I have given your notion considerable thought. It is an interesting idea, very interesting. To ask an actress—whose business it is to be charming—to coach young women in the ways of elegant behaviour is certainly a novel idea, and

I have turned my mind over and about a score of feminine thespians who might be at liberty to undertake such a task. It would require a very special person, you know. Talented enough to give satisfaction, not so old as to have forgotten what it is to be young, not so young as to be distracted from her duties by the likes of such as your handsome brother. Yes, a very special sort of person."

"I am prepared to pay, you know," Briony reminded him.

"Yes, I have not forgotten that. Certainly I know of many who would welcome the money, but somehow none seemed quite right for the task—until my mind lit up on one whom I believe may be the perfect person for you. It is perhaps an outrageous proposal—you shall decide—but before we go off upon this search, there is someone whom I would like you to meet. Not precisely what you had in mind but yet, but yet, possibly more suited to your task than anyone I could name."

"And this prodigy of perfection is . . . ?" asked Briony and was surprised to be rewarded with an amused smile.

"You do not know, miss, what you say, nor how close you are upon the mark."

"I fear I do not follow your thought, sir, but I place myself in your hands."

"Quite right, quite right," said Jarndyce jovially. "I cannot believe you will be sorry. At the very least you will have an amusing afternoon." He laughed quietly to himself. "Prodigy indeed!"

The part of London to which Mr. Jarndyce's carriage took them was quite near the center, but, in its shabbiness, might well have been far removed from the hustle and bustle of the city, the broad streets and handsome edifices of Mayfair and the newer sections springing up beyond St. James's. Here the streets were mean and narrow, the houses leaning against each other for mutual support. Briony was not overly concerned, since she knew that

Jarndyce would not have brought her here without safety, but Polly looked about apprehensively as if she expected a footpad to leap from the shadows and carry her away.

"It is not Bird Cage Walk, is it?" their Virgil asked. "Still there are worse places, by far, than this."

The carriage halted before a doorway much like the others except for one difference: the street before it had been neatly swept and the steps shone with scrubbing. Jarndyce mounted them with approval and rapped smartly upon the door with the knob of his stick. It was presently opened by a round woman in an apron and mobcap. She peered at him uncertainly before her face lightened with a cheery smile.

"Why, Mr. Jarndyce, isn't? Won't you come in, sir? Himself will be that pleased to see you, I am sure."

Jarndyce drew Briony forward. "Mrs. Biddy, may I present Miss Mitchem of Somerset?"

"Pleased and delighted, I am sure," said the householder. "Won't you please come this way?"

Mrs. Biddy was a plump little partridge of a woman with such a quick step that the others had to hurry as she scurried along before them past door after closed door in the twisting hallway.

"Mind your feet now, there's stairs ahead."

And there were: three up and three down which served no purpose now, though they once might have done. At length there was light ahead and with a quick turn they found themselves in a snug little sitting room with another short flight of steps at the far end.

Mrs. Biddy settled them comfortably in, dissuading Briony from a sagging chair and Mr. Jarndyce from one too narrow for his bulk. "If you will put yourselves at ease I will fetch both himself and a pot of something to drink." She smiled at Polly kindly. "Perhaps you would like to lend a bit of help?"

Polly looked at the householder doubtfully, but Briony urged her forward. It would do the country maid no harm to see how city people lived. It might even make her more content with her own lot at Mitchem Hall.

While they waited Briony took the opportunity of looking about the room, which, she saw, was oddly decorated with a variety of playbills and posters laid directly upon the wall and lightened here and there with framed lithographs, threepenny coloured prints and even one or two handsome engravings, though these were somewhat foxed from neglect and damp. She arose from her chair to examine them and saw that they were all in reference to one performer alone. Over and over was repeated the legend: "Master Biddy, the Young Roscius."

"Aye, well you may look," proclaimed a sonorous voice from behind her, "for I have played· them all, all the great roles: Hamlet, Romeo, Voltaire's Osman, Rolla in Sheridan's *Pizarro*, even Lear's fool. Notices you would not believe, and the coin rolling in like cheeses."

She turned to see that, standing on the flight of steps, poised in an attitude of dramatic attention and as tall and thin as six o'clock was the waiter from last evening. Now, however, as she looked at him, she realised how noble was the head set upon that skeletal frame. It was like the portrait bust of some old Roman, a senator or a forgotten emperor, magnificent in its vulpine glory.

"Miss Mitchem," said Jarndyce, "I have the great honour to present to you Mr. William Biddy.

"Will," he said to the man, "this lady may have work for you, so treat her well."

Briony looked at the manager in puzzlement. In her letter to him, she had asked to be introduced to some actress at liberty who might fit into her plans and serve as an instructress in the feminine arts. She had not thought to be made party to a jest such as this.

But Jarndyce, sensing her reluctance, waved reassuringly at the papered walls. "As you can see," he said, "Mr. Biddy has been upon the boards for many years, despite his youth." And Briony, looking more closely, saw that their host was, perhaps, younger than she had suspected. Scarcely older, in fact, than herself. Somewhere between twenty-five and thirty, she judged, although those distinctive features had at first suggested otherwise.

He had been standing in his stance of easy confidence all this time, but now he came to the foot of the stair and made his way to her, moving with dignity and an utmost economy of movement, a natural elegance in his bearing.

"Yes," he said mournfully, "I have played them all—or, rather, 'the Young Roscius' played them. I often have the notion that that young boy and I are completely different entities. His was all the glory and mine the ashes. When I think of it, I am often puzzled that I cannot remember what it was like. Imagine a lad of thirteen and fourteen holding at bay the audience of Covent Garden. Incredible!" Then he brightened considerably.

"But I have a good life, you know. I play occasionally and Mrs. Biddy coddles me. I only regret that I do not more often find outlet for my talents."

"Well, my friend, that is why we have come to you," Jarndyce said, "for I am well aware that you have more hats to wear than that of an actor."

"What do you mean, sir?"

Jarndyce diplomatically and briefly explained what it was that Miss Mitchem required. The former prodigy knit his noble brow, considered, then assented gracefully.

"Yes, that is something I could bring myself to do for a pair of months." From his height he looked down at Briony with a quizzical expression. "But you, I suspect from your hesitation, have doubts in the matter, what? I do not altogether blame you, but let me assure you that my wide—oh, very wide—range of experience has prepared me to do everything in the theatre arts. I have been prompter, scene maker, carpenter, wardrobe man, property man, scene changer, actor, and, yes, even actress upon occasion."

Briony half-opened her mouth to speak, but he held her

off with an upraised finger. "Wait," and, whipping a shawl from the back of a chair where it had been carelessly discarded, he flew back up the little stair, disappearing from sight for a moment's time only.

Then, before Briony's eyes appeared a spectral figure at the top of the steps; Lady Macbeth, complete with candle, the shawl thrown loosely about her head and shoulders. All was suggested, not so much by costume or property as by the genius of the actor himself in making Briony see, even before he spoke, who the portrayal was to be.

"Yet here's a spot," he murmured, seeming to examine the free hand in the nonexistent candlelight.

"Out damned spot! Out I say!" He listened to a clock perhaps tolling in his brain. "One . . . two . . . Why, then, 'tis time to do it." And then to another: "Fie, my lord, fie! A soldier and afeard?" The contemptuous laughter would have withered flowers. "What need we fear who knows it, when none can call our power to account?"

But now there was something further. A horrified revulsion. "Yet who would have thought the old man had so much blood in him?"

"Do you follow my thought?" whispered Jarndyce.

"The thane of Fife had a wife. Where is *she* now?" asked Lady Macbeth through the genius of Mr. Biddy. "What?— Will these hands ne'er be clean?"

Certainly it was true, Briony could see, that Mr. Biddy had transcended not only himself and his appearance but his very sex to bring the horrid woman to life, washing her hands in a futile gesture, holding a palm up to her distended nostrils as if to scent putrefaction.

"Here's the smell of blood still. All the perfumes of Arabia," she predicted, "will not sweeten this little hand."

And in the eyes of his audience Biddy was what he proclaimed—a frail, lovely, and distraught woman.

"Oh!" she cried. "Oh, oh!"

The spectral figure gracefully crossed the floor toward them, speaking into the air, addressing some unseen companion.

"Wash your hands. Put on your nightgown. Look not so pale! I tell you yet again, Banquo's buried. He cannot come out on's grave!"

"Well?" asked Jarndyce, sotto voce.

"To bed, to bed!" cried the tragedy queen, retreating. "Come, come! Come. Come, give me your hand. To bed, to bed, to bed!"

As the mad figure disappeared again at the stair-top, Briony could not help applauding, and Jarndyce joined her in it. "How wonderful!" she cried enthusiastically. "He made me believe him—even though my mind told me it was not possible."

"You see?" asked the theatre manager. Briony saw for the first time what was his intention.

"You are suggesting that I employ *him* as the coach I require for the young women?" She giggled at the thought of it. "Oh, but that is impossible."

"Why? Because he is a man?" Jarndyce asked. "He has more talent and vision than any performer I know."

"Then why can you not put him to work?" she asked reasonably.

"I do, as often as I can. That is what I am trying to do now."

"Put him to work at my expense? I can justify much to my employers, I imagine, but not a man to teach girls how to be women."

"Somehow I had believed better of you," Jarndyce said sadly.

Polly came bursting back into the room—but such a changed Polly! Where before she had been dressed in typical servant's woolsey, ill-fitting and drab, she now seemed as smartly turned-out in her way as Briony herself.

"Oh, miss, you see what she has done? Ain't it fine, miss?" The girl whirled before Briony. "You do not mind, do you, Miss Mitchem? They are the same clothes, you know. She only . . . only adjusted them a bit, you see."

Briony could, indeed, see that such was the case. Someone had performed what seemed to her a near miracle in transforming a shapeless garment into one which was quite stylish. She could see that it was only a matter of a few tucks and darts, a bit of trimming, but the difference was immeasurable.

"Why, how wonderful!" she said without thought. "Who on earth accomplished it?"

Mrs. Biddy appeared in the door at the bottom of the stairs. "Here, come back, girl! Those basting stitches won't hold if you go bouncing about like that."

"Is this your work?" asked Briony.

Mrs. Biddy looked down her nose. "Well, I hope you don't think I done wrong, miss? It seemed a pity to make the child wear it the way it was, when it would take so little to set it right. I can rip it all out again, if you insist I do."

"No, no. It is wonderful. Tell me, do you do this for a living? Are you a seamstress?"

Mrs. Biddy sniffed and shook her head proudly. "Not a mere seamstress, miss. When I hire out, I go as wardrobe mistress or not at all. I have my reputation to think of, and there is no pay in being a mere sewer, if you follow me."

"I do. I do follow." In Briony's mind's eye appeared Anne Barstow's expensive but ill-fitting travelling costume. She suspected it was typical of the young woman's wardrobe in its entirety.

"Are you engaged at the moment? Would you be free to take on a two-month commission?"

Mrs. Biddy looked somewhat taken aback at the suddenness of the proposition. "Would it be nearby, miss? I have Mr. Biddy to think of, you see. He is a most accomplished man, but he seems to be able to do naught for himself. Like a babby he is in requiring to be looked after."

"Actually," Briony laughed as she caught Jarndyce's knowing eye, "it is not at all nearby, but I don't doubt we can work something out."

=8=

HOLLYMEAD HOUSE, BRIONY had found when she inspected it, was in the lovely Vale of Taunton Dean. Elizabethan in conception, it had the look of having been altered by every owner for two hundred years, and such was almost truly the case. Expanded under James the First, it had been partially burned by the Roundheads and been restored by one of Cromwell's aides, who took it as spoils; the restoration was then altered by a leman of Charles II who received it as compensation for a broken heart. A new front was added in the reign of Queen Anne, and the park enclosed in the year the Hanovers succeeded to the throne by quite a different sort of mistress, from her portrait a tall beanpole, imported from Germany by George I. The gardens were laid out by Harmony Partridge in the following reign, a task so expensive (a hill was removed and a lake newly invented) that at that owner's death it passed into the hands of agents and solicitors. It was now let—furnished and staffed—at a very good price for long-term occupancy. Briony had no idea what was currently being paid, but the rent would undoubtedly be high for such a short term. It seemed to her evident that the principals for whom the Graf von Ahlden acted were possessed of very deep pockets into which the count could dip.

Despite his previous acquiescence, Redmond was unhappy to be there. He had moped morosely about the house during their inspection of it, complaining about the lack of a suitable space for his painting, and now returned to his previous plaint.

"I still don't see what you think you can accomplish in a mere eight weeks," he complained. "You will only have begun when you come to the end of it. And you'll never in this world make a difference to that pickle-barrel."

"If you are speaking of Isabella, you have no right to be so rude. I have great hopes for her. Sensible eating and Mr. Biddy's training may accomplish wonders. And, you know, I am counting on you for more than drawing lessons. Both young women need to have something in their lives outside their experience until now. I hope that you will provide a part of that."

"Good Lord, I hope you don't mean to say that I am to be a school prize?"

He continued to grouse about the grounds while she discussed plans and schedules with the permanent staff and with the Biddys. He poked glumly into outbuildings and sheds, hoping to come across something, anything, that would be suitable for use as a studio. He needed not only a place in which to paint, but a haven to which he could retreat from the women with whom he would be cooped up for these two months in an even more stringent way than during the rest of the year at the academy.

During an interval in the making of the larger arrangements, Briony joined him, unwilling to accept his rejection of every possible spot.

"What about one of the turrets? The light would be good."

"Too small. Not enough room to breathe."

"Then what of that handsome room on the floor just above your own chamber? It has a northern exposure."

"Far too large. I should rattle about like a pea."

"Come, come, Redmond, there must be somewhere suitable. It is only for two months, as you yourself have pointed out."

They were walking along a flagged passage beyond the

kitchen and scullery, opening doors on either side to reveal endless storerooms and cellars, when Briony called out in genuine surprise. "Oh, my, brother, just look what we have here."

Redmond, peering past her shoulder into the cool empty chamber, could not see that it was anything out of the ordinary except that it was blessed with light and was very long, larger than a ballroom, and had very high ceilings. Across it, on a sagging rope, was strung a net of widely woven mesh. On the walls, in various strategic spots, were painted bull's-eyes.

"Will this do for painting?" his sister asked.

He brushed the question aside. "Painting? Don't you know what this is? A court room for royal tennis. We had one at Ordway. Have you never heard of it?"

She had *heard* of tennis, of course, but only as the sport of monarchs such as Henry Tudor. "Is it still played?" she asked. Foolishly, because he had just said there had been such a court at his school, and since the net still hung in place.

Redmond poked about enthusiastically. "I wonder if there are racquets about?"

"We can ask the butler," promised his sister, gratified to see the change in his attitude. She did not understand how he hoped to play alone a game requiring two, but she had no intention of saying so. La, he might want her to learn the sport, and she had enough ahead of her as it was.

Curiously, with the prospect of recreation in view, however solitary, Redmond accepted the idea of his shared responsibility with greater grace.

"But you must allow that my evenings are my own," he stipulated.

Briony was firm. It was especially in the evenings that the presence of a handsome young man would be invaluable. "You shall have the mornings to do with as you like. You may paint or rove the countryside, even sleep if you choose, but I shall expect that you will be clean, properly dressed, and at the luncheon table every day and prepared to spend the remainder of it as my assistant."

He groaned but agreed. "I have always found the morning light best for painting, anyway," he confessed.

The removal from Mitchem House to Hollymead was made during the last week of June, and the young women arrived on the morning of the following Monday. Mr. Barstow, who accompanied Anne, looked about him with evident relish.

"Aye, now here's the sort of place makes one to stop and wonder, by all!"

"But I am sure you have great houses in your part of the world, do you not, sir?" Briony asked.

"Oh, aye, but they are mingy and mean compared to this. A man would have to be a roaring success indeed to own such a place as this."

"And are you not such a success, Mr. Barstow?" Briony very slightly raised her eyebrows in amused interrogation.

He considered, a look of comprehension dawning in his face. "Why, perhaps I am, miss. Perhaps I am, after all." He flushed self-consciously. "Tha must understand, miss, that a lad from a two-room cot in a drab village must look high to think of himself living in such a place."

His daughter, however, seemed to take it in easy stride. To her, it seemed, great or small, a house was a shelter from the rain and cold, a place to sleep and to scrub. She accepted the mansion, the furnishings, and the staff with complete lack of pretension. Even the faintly scornful expression on the face of the maid who unpacked her boxes and put her things away passed unnoticed by the ironmaster's daughter. She was friendly and, though socially unschooled, generally unassuming with little save her accent to unlearn. Quite different from the other pupil.

From the beginning Isabella, who had professed herself eager to cooperate in all things, proved that old habits died hard. Raised in seclusion and surrounded only by servants, she still had a carryover of her old manner. It was hardly surprising since all things had been granted by her doting attendants, but it had not, by any means, educated her in the wisdom of charm. She was at once insecure and over-assertive; reclusive by nature, yet desiring above all things to be readied for the great role she had so surprisingly been delegated to play. She conducted herself in a slightly imperious way, and from the beginning the staff responded with a quality of service never afforded any previous tenant, a case of "expect and ye shall receive."

"She may be a cow," opined the footman when sitting down to table in the servants' hall, "but she is quality, mark my words."

"Quality or no, she'll have no special treatment from me," said cook firmly. "I have my orders concerning her, and I expect to follow 'em. That Miss Mitchem, she knows a thing or two and, if you'll take my advice, you'll do as she tells you to do. No special favours on the sly.

"And no taking of bribes, neither," she added darkly. "Miss Mitchem pays us all enough to bypass extras."

"Bribes?" asked the footman indignantly. "As if I would!"

To be served with a plain chop and vegetable while the others at table were offered a variety of succulent foods (some of which, intended expressly for Miss Barstow, required a passable dexterity in eating skills) was easy enough for Isabella to accept, but when the dessert course was served, the princess found it politic to excuse herself. This worked well enough for the first two or three days, but when Miss Mitchem began requesting that she remain until the others had done (and, meeting with resistance, then insisted), Isabella found her patience tested. She saw no reason for such a stricture and merely ignored it, leaving when she chose.

It meant, she found, that the next day she was not called at all. When she found that she was to be given her supper on a tray, she brusquely summoned Briony to her chamber and demanded an explanation.

"Why, I had thought that since you did not regard us with enough courtesy to remain until the meal was done," said Briony coolly, "you may as well dine alone and save both your feelings and ours. Your tray will arrive shortly, I am sure."

"I will make the decisions in such things," Isabella informed her. "In future I will inform cook of my pleasure in the matter. As for this evening, I shall have my tray here, as you suggest. Please be sure that it includes a sweet. A tart, perhaps, or trifle. I need the sweetness to aid my digestion."

When the tray arrived it bore only a chop, soup, and a pot of tea; less by far than she had dined on the previous day. When the princess saw it, her petulance came to the fore. Lifting the tray bodily from the table where it had been placed by the maid, she threw it, teapot and all, against the wall. The yellow fluid trickled down the brocade, irretrievably marring the fabric. Briony, who had been waiting in the corridor for just such a reaction, stepped back inside.

"You will oblige me by clearing up after yourself," she said in just such a colourless voice as she sometimes used with the young ladies of Mitchem Academy. She had some time ago discovered that such a passionless approach sometimes succeeded where a more personal reaction failed.

But in this instance it had no effect whatsoever. Instead, Isabella merely looked at her in well-bred fury for several moments before she realised that her instructress meant exactly what she said. She, Isabella Wittelsbach, Princess of Schleswig-Holstein-Gundorp-Thoningen, was expected to demean herself to the extent of stooping to retrieve shards of broken crockery and congealing food. With tightened jaw and a face pale with anger she swept past Briony and flung open the door. The oath she spat as she did so was one she had not learned in the polite salons of Europe. Furiously, she made her way through the house until she found the servants' hall. Cook regarded her with only mild interest.

"Is there aught I can do for you, miss?"

Isabella looked wildly about. "I will have some of this, some of this, and some of this," she announced, pointing at food the woman was just setting out.

"That is the servants' dinner, miss."

Isabella's eyes blazed. "Then the servants in this house are treated a great deal better than the guests."

Cook was unperturbed. "You must speak to Miss Mitchem, miss, for any change of your meals and portions. I have no authority to change the instructions she has given me."

She smiled rather grimly, pleased to at least have the authority to outface this spotty but imperious young woman. "In any case, miss, I have already sent your supper to your chamber on a tray. I expect if you step quickly, you will find it has not gotten too cold by now."

Isabella's mouth tightened. "Am I to understand that you are refusing me? Defying me?"

"Yes, miss," said cook imperturbably, "if that is how you like to put it. I have my orders, and I mean to follow them."

Isabella was increasingly conscious of the fact that more than one pair of eyes was watching her. When she looked covertly about, the servants became increasingly busy with their tasks, but she was uncomfortably aware that she was making rather a spectacle of herself, and she tried another tack.

"I fear there was a slight accident with the tray," she said. "The clumsy girl who brought it set it unevenly on the table, and it overturned onto the floor."

"Is that a fact, miss? What a pity. I expect it made rather a mess."

"Yes," said Isabella, feeling she was at last making some headway. " I would appreciate it if you would send someone to clear it away."

"Oh, I have no authority for that, miss. The one to speak to is Miss Mitchem. I daresay she will deal with it properly."

Isabella bit her lip. As she turned about in annoyance, her eyes fell upon a young woman cleaning silver. "You there, be good enough to go to my room and clear up the mess your fellow made."

The servant girl's eyes sought those of cook, who shook her head imperceptibly. The servant's eyes dropped, and she went on with her busy polishing as if Isabella had not spoken.

"No," said cook, "Lily has her own work to do. You cannot expect her to do it and someone else's as well. It isn't fair, is it, miss? Whoever made the mess should clear it away. I expect if you speak to Miss Mitchem, she will agree."

Isabella's eyes seemed to throw sparks, and she looked for a brief moment as if she might strike the woman who was opposing her. Instead she raised her chin and walked out of the room, closing the door of the servants' hall firmly behind her.

Cook's eyes rolled heavenward. "I hope Miss Mitchem knows what she is about and that is for true."

All the way upstairs Isabella fumed, and when she reached her chamber, she found the little maidservant was gone but that Miss Mitchem sat in a chair by the window, placidly gazing out over the lawn. The dishes and tray were still where they had fallen, and Isabella realised that her outburst had won her nothing at all.

"I had believed that my chamber was my own," she said icily. "If it is otherwise, please be so good as to tell me."

Briony arose from the chair and faced her highness with unruffled calm. She was not as tall nor as regal as the princess, but she knew that, in this instance, she held the reins of authority.

"There is a principle I imagine you might do well to contemplate," she said evenly. "It concerns the question of what is due from a highly born person to her less well-placed associates: noblesse oblige, the obligations of nobility."

Isabella flared her nostrils haughtily. "Such rules do not apply to servants."

"Until the summer is gone, we are all equals here," Briony answered. "That was agreed in the beginning. If that is not so, all else will fail."

"Those who are paid for their services have no claim to equality," Isabella sneered. She knew she was endangering her own position, even her own progress, but she could not stop the rush, could not hold her tongue from enunciating the words that sprang so easily to it.

"You are as much a servant as the kitchen maid, madame," she said. "I would be within my right to dismiss you for insolence."

For the first time, Briony allowed a thin smile to touch her lips as she recognised the girl's insecurity and the interior turmoil which prompted her words. Heaven only knew what indignities had been forced upon her as the plain daughter of a minor German nobleman whose reputation as a disciplinarian was well known. With this breach everything was on schedule.

"Will your highness not consider your own position?" she asked.

"You need not appeal to my good nature," said Isabella coldly. "It will not save you if I should leave."

"No, your highness, but what will you have gained? Your own situation is more perilous than mine."

Perhaps no one had ever spoken so forthrightly to the young woman before; perhaps no one had dared. It had not been said in a taunting way, but kindly, and the very kindness struck home like a dart. She bit her lip, turning away toward the window and staring out over the great lawn as the tears welled from her eyes and ran down her cheeks.

Briony watched the battle from behind the princess's

back, understanding that the girl struggled with her own nature. She saw the spine straighten, the shoulders tense and then straighten as well, squaring proudly.

Isabella grew very still. This was the moment, her governess suspected, when she would either reject whatever aid might come to her from Briony Mitchem or would consent to be ruled for her own sake and that of her future. The plump hands balled themselves into fists, and Briony guessed that her gamble had been lost. In a moment the obese young woman would turn around again, demanding Briony's own capitulation.

From the wide green expanse of the lawn below drifted up a cheerful whistle which Briony recognised at once. It was Redmond expressing himself with a warbled rendition of his favourite tune: "The Jolly Miller's Daughter." He, at least, would not be displeased that the experiment had come to naught. Isabella seemed to have heard it as well, for she relaxed a little, peering through the curtain at the young man as he passed beneath her, sketchbook in hand, on his way toward the stream and the bending willows that edged the park.

As Briony watched, the young woman drew a deep, shuddery breath and turned back into the room. Avoiding the eyes of the schoolmistress, she crossed to the jumble of food and crockery on the floor and, kneeling, placed it bit by bit upon the tray, and the tray upon the table.

"Please," she said to Briony, "would you say to cook that I do not care for any further supper, but enquire whether I might have watercress sandwiches for tomorrow's luncheon?"

Smiling and almost in tears herself, Briony embraced her. The princess stiffened and began to draw herself away. For the instant of a heartbeat Briony was afraid that she had, after all, lost the battle. Then she felt the princess's body relax and her own embrace tentatively returned.

They had come to the end of the beginning.

= 9 =

"No, no, Miss Isabella, if you please! Head up, back very straight, if you please! Do not glide, miss, if you please! Keep the steps short and even, Miss Anne. Try for balance, miss, if you please, so that you will not sway. The walk should be regal, young ladies, yet natural."

Isabella bit her tongue to keep from making a rebelliously "regal" remark, then cool-headedness prevailed. Was this not what she wanted, after all; an opportunity to alter, to make herself over, hidden from the eyes of the small, backbiting German court where she had grown up? Without the unkindly clever remarks and the backbiting and sniggering behind the fans. She carefully straightened the volume of Fanny Burney's *Camilla* on her head and concentrated on keeping her steps short and even. She received her reward.

"That is right, Miss Isabella. That is right. Excellent!"

In the fortnight since her sword-crossing with Miss Mitchem, the princess had, dispassionately, divined a few small alterations in herself. No miraculous overnight transformation was to be expected, but her complexion was beginning to clear and her dresses fit a bit less snugly than when she had arrived. She could see that there were changes in Miss Barstow as well. The ironmonger's daughter had been involved in long conferences with Mr. Biddy's wife, emerging with a simpler, far more elegant look, which Isabella vastly envied, though she knew, however much she tried, it would be beyond her.

Anne Barstow's voice, however, was still the shrill peacock cry it had always been, the accent and idiom of the border country still lying heavily upon it. Despite Mr. Biddy's patient coaching, it seemed not to have altered at all.

"*Lift* the words, Miss Anne, *lift* the words on the breath. Carry them forward without forcing, if you please. No, no, do not forget to breathe, miss. You cannot speak at all if you do not breathe."

Isabella's accent in English had been perfected by a long line of nannies, governesses, and tutors. It was peculiar, she had always thought, that though neither of her parents claimed more than a distant cousinship with the Hanovers of England, she had always been taught to speak English not as a second language, but with an equal status to Thoningen's German. The result was that her command of it was idiomatic and pleasingly natural. She marvelled, therefore, that an actual inhabitant of the country should make such a hard job of it. It was especially tragic in a woman of such obvious beauty and charm as her schoolmate. Isabella felt no envy of the ironmaster's daughter in that respect. It was Miss Barstow herself who brought the matter of language forward in conversation.

"Ah, Miss Isabella, if only you could borrow me a bit of your way with the language!" she cried wistfully one afternoon.

"If you could only *lend* . . ." Isabella corrected automatically. "If only you could *lend* me language, not borrow."

It was obvious that Anne Barstow misunderstood her. "Nay, why would you wish to have my tongue?"

Isabella clarified her meaning, and Anne nodded eagerly. "Oh, aye, I have always said it at home. It is what we *say* there, you see."

"I am sure you do," the princess said, and even she recognised how kindly she meant it, "but it is not said in better society." She paused diffidently. "And there is another thing—if you do not take offence at my saying it?"

"Nay, you must say what pleases you, if it will help me."

"Well, then," Isabella went on, "do you understand what Mr. Biddy *means* by 'on the breath'?"

Red-faced, Anne shook her head. "And I try, you know I do, but I only get all puffy."

Isabella squeezed her shoulder. "Never mind. My singing teacher at home always used those words with me, and I was very puzzled until I screwed up enough courage to ask for a demonstration of what he meant."

"*You* were too shy to ask? *That* I cannot believe."

Isabella giggled. "You can imagine! I do not suppose anyone cares to play the fool, and I had the added burden of being . . . " She stopped in mid-sentence, recalling that for now she was no one, was incognito, a plain Miss Wittlesbach. "I had this burden of being so very heavy," she amended. "It made me quite diffident.

"Here, let me show you. Take a deep breath." (Anne sucked in the air with great vigour.) "Hold it for a moment, then let it out slowly as you speak."

To her credit, Anne tried to follow the instruction, but only succeeded in growing very red in the face. The words emerged with all the force of an air gun. Isabella laughed, Anne looked taken aback, then both giggled as if they were engaged in a game.

"Here, try it *this* way, if you please, Miss Anne," said a voice from behind them. It was Mr. Biddy. "You have anticipated me, Miss Isabella, by beginning Miss Anne's lesson for tomorrow." His tone was so bright that it was evident there was no ill-feeling behind his words.

Taking a candle from a sideboard, he carefully lit it. Holding it up before Miss Barstow, he said, "Take a deep breath again, if you please, miss, but very slowly. That is right, very slowly. Pause for a moment, if you please. Now, let it out again as slowly as you took it in."

The candle flame flickered wildly as she did so, but he was as patient as usual.

"Again, please, miss. Say your name very slowly, letting

your breath carry it out of you. Try not to make the flame flicker at all." Anne scooped in the air. "No, no, slowly." She drew it in again. He held up a finger.

"Very well, now, Miss Anne. 'My name is Anne Barstow.' Say it without disturbing the flame."

"My . . . name . . . is . . . Anne . . . BARSTOW." The remaining breath, well-modulated until then, puffed out and the candle flame waved violently. All three laughed, but Anne, more encouraged, was more than ready to begin again.

"My . . . name . . . is . . . Anne . . . Barrr . . . stowww," she enunciated carefully. The light hardly flickered.

"Again," said Biddy. "More quickly."

"My name is Anne BARstow." It fluctuated wildly.

"On the breath, miss," he cautioned. "On the breath." But now she knew what it was he meant.

"My name is Anne Bar-stow." Scarcely a flicker.

"Fine. Now enunciate as you say it."

Anne raised her eyebrows, questioning. "Please?"

"Say each syllable very carefully," Isabella explained.

"My . . . naame . . . is . . . Aaanne . . . Baar . . . stowww." The flame stood tall and straight.

"Excellent!" cried Mr. Biddy, and the flame fled to one side of the wick, causing much merriment among them. "One more time and listen carefully to yourself."

"My name is Anne Barstow." The voice emerged, rich and full. "Oh, I can hear it. My name is Anne Barstow. My name is Anne Barstow." She was almost on the edge of tears. "My name *is* Anne Barstow!" And the flame wavered not at all.

"Fifteen minutes by the clock each day," instructed Mr. Biddy. The young woman enthusiastically agreed.

"And you, Miss Isabella—chin high, shoulders back, and spine straight. One half-hour by the clock. Each must watch the other. Listen to the other. You will benefit from each other's attention, eh? You will do well together."

Isabella's attention, though, was often diverted, for every morning she saw Redmond slipping away to a group of outbuildings near the kitchen and scullery. Often he would be gone until it was time to prepare for luncheon and the beginning of his working day.

It must be explained that will-he, nill-he, Redmond was working his familiar magic over at least one of the students. Anne Barstow seemed impervious to his slightly rakish youthful charm, but Isabella, who had never been on a level of anything approaching the easy familiarity she was allowed at Hollymead, found the novelty enchanting. It must also be said, of course, that Redmond had no idea of the havoc he caused in the heart of the princess. Had he known, unfortunately, he would have dismissed the knowledge with a shudder at the worst, or a look of sad regret at the best. To the young artist, she offered nothing at all. Had he known of her nobility, of course, things might have been different. Or, again, they might not, for never yet had a girl attracted him who was not slim and elegant. And, Redmond being Redmond, even they were of limited interest to him.

It was on a Tuesday that Isabella's curiosity overcame her, and she covertly followed the young artist when he slipped away. It was not that she had not thought of it earlier, but she had, quite honestly, been afraid. Redmond affected her in a way no young man had ever done before. Nothing had ever encouraged her in that direction; even in minor German courts young women of the sort she had become are not admired. But the dawning of an awareness of oneself can be a beautiful thing, especially when it is entwined with first love and hope.

Not that she thought of any of this as she crept along a flagstone corridor from which opened a series of closed wooden doors. What would Redmond be doing here? He must have gone on through to the other end and out, mustn't he? Then from behind one of the doors came an oddly disturbing sound—an oddly familiar *slap! slap!* Intrigued, she pushed against the door. It resisted, and she pushed harder. The door swung open beneath her weight, and she all but fell into the room.

Redmond, his shirt of ruffled lawn open at the throat, the sleeves turned back, was swatting a ball of wrapped cloth so that it rebounded off the walls. From the way it sprang back, Isabella surmised that at its center was a core of caoutchouc or India rubber. She watched him for several moments before a glancing blow bounced the ball off the wall near the door. He retrieved it awkwardly and seemed almost ashamed to have been caught at his game.

"Oh, hello!" he called out. She could not tell from his expression whether he was annoyed or not.

"Have you been in here before?" She shook her head. "It is called a tennis court," he explained.

"Yes. We have one in Thoningen."

"Thoningen? Is that your home? Where is that?"

"Near Hanover. It is in the confederation."

"Really? I don't think I have ever heard of it."

"It is very small," she admitted. "But we have a tennis court."

"And you have played, have you?"

"Once or twice. I am not very good."

He laughed at her frank admission. "To tell the truth, neither am I. I only come here and knock the ball around for exercise." A pleasant thought seemed to strike him. "I say, would you like to play a bit? The butler found me two racquets."

"Would your sister approve?"

Privately, from what he had heard his sister say, he suspected that Briony would approve any activity which would stir Miss Wittlesbach from the library of Hollymead, where she seemed to retreat during much of her free time.

"It is rather strenuous, you know," he warned her.

"Yes, I know. I have watched my brothers play it a good deal."

He seemed rather excited by that. "Have you? Perhaps you can give me some pointers."

He tugged at the sagging net and managed to draw it more or less taut. "If Briony allows us to go on, I shall have to do something with this." He loosened his hold, and the net began to sag once more.

"Your knot is wrong," she advised him and deftly pulled the net back to its proper tension, then deftly manoeuvered the cord to hold it in place. He looked at her with a gleam of new respect.

"Very well, are you ready?" He tossed her the other racquet. "En garde!" It did not seem quite the expression to use, but it served well enough in this case.

They were neither of them very skilled; Isabella perhaps a bit more than Redmond, but she did not allow it to show too boldly. Nevertheless, it was amusing enough that at the end of play, they agreed to meet again the following morning if Isabella could escape her posture exercises and drill from Mr. Biddy. Within a day or two it had become a settled routine, part of their usual day.

When Briony learned of it, she was amused, for it suited her plans more completely than any persuasion of Redmond on her part could have done. She was equally happy, as well, that the bearer of the infatuation was Isabella, already betrothed to a great man of Europe, rather than Anne Barstow, whose father might not appreciate a match between his daughter and a penniless young aristocrat.

— 10 —

THE DAYS PASSED QUIETLY, but it was becoming a source of mild irritation to Briony of late that both the count and the ironmaster deemed it necessary to visit Hollymead far more often than she thought wise. There was certainly valid reason for them to be concerned over the progress of the experiment, but she feared that their very presence was likely to prove a disturbing influence. Anne Barstow, for example, did very well when no visitors were about, or even when engaged in conversation by the count. Mr. Biddy had done wonders with her, and his wife had turned her into quite a creature of fashion, but whenever her father reappeared she dropped back into the old ways. She laughingly spoke of her father as "hulver-headed" when she meant "hard-headed," and Briony once even heard her refer to luncheon as "pudding-time," though, to her credit, she immediately realised her faux pas and guiltily clapped a hand over her mouth. It seemed, as well, to Briony that when the Graf von Ahlden was present, Isabella's demeanour had a disturbing tendency to become clumsy and defensive.

And there was something else which alarmed her even more. She could not be sure, yet, if it were merely her fancy or not, but it seemed to her that, when he was present, the count's attention wandered far more often from his charge to Miss Barstow. The more elegant her mode of dress, the more adept she became at social discourse, the more interested he seemed to become. Briony took it upon herself to see that they were rarely together, which called for an exercise of ingenuity on her part. Over a period of time, she saw what she believed was a growing annoyance on the part of the count at her interference, but she believed it preferable to an even stronger reaction from the ironmaster should he come to think that the nobleman was trifling with the affections of his beloved daughter. There was a chance, albeit a slim one, that such was not at all the case, but Briony saw no reason to abandon precaution. Comparing the situations of the two young women, she came to see that it was one thing that the princess might engage in a one-sided infatuation (for Briony had no doubt there was no response on her brother's part) which might, in the long run, even prove beneficial, but that it was quite another to allow a sheltered, completely unsophisticated girl to be swept away by the bearing and elan of a continental nobleman. There must be some way, she hoped, to curtail the count's visits.

Actually, the ironmaster, too, appeared to find that he had frequent business in the neighbourhood. Most often, she gathered, it was with Mayor Dedham and it seemed to follow that, whenever Barstow had business in Hadrian's Green, he must also come to Hollymead. This was all very well, except that he seemed to come not as a visitor, but almost as a settled occupant. If Briony sent word that she was engaged and unable to give him an interview, he wandered about the house and grounds until she was free, or until he located his daughter, thereby distracting Anne from her studies and unconsciously luring her backward to old habits. If his daughter was not available, he took up an easy conversation with anyone who was at hand. That this might be a servant bothered him not in the least, but the staff, she found, were not so sanguine.

"Servants is servants, miss, and masters is masters," as cook explained when bringing the matter to Briony's attention. "There is such a thing as pride of place, you know, and we are not accustomed to being put upon an equal footing. We has our own ways—our likes and dislikes, y'might say—same as anybody. It iddn't right, somehow, that we be forced to mingle with the likes of Mr. Barstow, fine though he may be, when we has our own work to do."

Briony had never taken the trouble to look outward from this perspective, but she found it both piquant and amusing. Anne's father certainly fit into no defined category of society, and if he spanned the classes, he certainly did so without conscious thought or effort. Obviously, he had no inkling that English servants are the most conservative people in the world, horrified at the breakdown of barriers which protected as much as confined them. If they had no personal inclination to cross over, they found it equally distressing that others should feel free to trespass within their precincts.

"And another thing, miss, though I don't like to mention it, would it be possible to let me know how many they is for dinner of a day? I prides myself on the board I set forth, but it do become difficult if I cannot judge."

"I see exactly," Briony agreed. It was obvious that the time had come to put her foot down in the matter of unexpected guests. It might be a pleasant diversion for the men, but it was scarcely worth the disruption.

She bided her time for a week until the two men were present at the same time, then asked them to join her in the library.

"Gentlemen," she said simply, "I fear that I must cease being hostess and assume the role of schoolmistress with you as well as with the young ladies. I find that I must say something that, although unpleasant, is in the best interests of all of us."

The Graf von Ahlden, already perhaps piqued at her behaviour toward him despite his rank and position, responded with an upraised eyebrow. "I do hope, Miss Mitchem, that we are not to be sent supperless to bed?"

She nodded pleasantly. "Something of the sort, I fear. It

comes to this: While I am always happy to see you and Mr. Barstow, glad to rearrange my work to allow you an appointment, I fear that your frequent visits have an adverse effect upon the young ladies."

She went on to disclose her observations, to praise the young women for their enormous progress, all the while trying to retain a businesslike, pedagogical tone.

"I believe, you see, gentlemen, that you are not really perceiving Anne and Isabella as the creatures they are fast becoming, but with the inattentive eyes of the past. You see them still as the young women you brought me, but they are working hard to transform themselves. I would not wish to change that."

"Are you saying, miss, that we are doing harm by coming here to the girls?" the ironmaster asked. He scratched his head. "I never considered that. You're saying I am *bad* for my own girl? That I must not see her, not even come here to where she is?"

The count, with an eye toward the satisfaction of his superiors, reluctantly agreed that it was possible, just possible, mind you, that well enough should be left alone, but the ironmaster seemed fairly stricken.

Briony took a deep breath and tried to explain her position as rationally as possible. "It really is for her own good, Mr. Barstow. Anne must learn to break old habits as she acquires new ones."

"I had it in mind that my girl should be polished a bit to move in society, miss," he growled crossly. "I had no notion she was to be turned against her own kin. What sort of woman can you be, I wonder?"

"I hope I am sensible enough, sir, not to take offence at your words. Your daughter is a fine young woman, and you, I have no doubt, are an upstanding man. Certainly you have lifted yourself up from the position to which you were born."

Sensing, perhaps, that a storm was in the making, the

Graf von Ahlden excused himself and quietly left the room. No sooner had the door closed discreetly behind him than Barstow repeated his question.

"So, am I to be looked down upon because I made my own way?" The question was almost a taunt, certainly it was filled with defiance. But Briony rose to the challenge in an unexpected way.

"You astound me, sir! Truly you do. The truth is quite to the contrary; I believe what you have done is admirable." She fancied he blinked at that. "But," she continued, "do you wish to hold your daughter to the level you have achieved? She has not the physical ingenuity nor any trade to draw her up in the way you advanced yourself, only her sweet nature and the beginnings of a great beauty. Both are great assets, but commonness of speech and manner will inevitably hold her back. When you sought me out I had believed we were in agreement, but I see that I was mistaken."

He had cooled enough to dispute this. "Nay, lass, we are in agreement, and I can see that you have done wonders with Annie already, but I did not think my girl was to be improved all out of my own society. I love her and I wish the best for her, but I cannot lose her, do you ken?"

Briony's heart went out to him as she saw how clumsy she had been in stressing her point. She involuntarily put out her hand to touch his arm. "And you think so little of your daughter as to believe she would ever be ashamed of the man who has so loved her? But she will marry one day, you know."

He sighed heavily. "Aye, I know. If I had only had the courage to send her away to school when she was smaller, I should not be fashing myself with all this now."

Thoughtfully, he rose and wandered toward the window. "I am sure, miss, that you've the interests of Annie at heart, and now I see that I have been a bit . . ." His voice trailed, and Briony regarded him curiously. He was staring out of the window with a strangely fixed and intent expression. Then, without turning his head or altering the direction of his gaze, he spoke to her quietly.

"Come over here beside me, miss, if you please. Naturally, if you see, with no rapid movements. We have a bird in the brake, and we do not want it to be frightened away."

She came forward curiously. "There in the thicket, do you see?" he asked.

But she could detect no more than the afternoon sun on the leaves, which she was about to admit when the slightest flicker of movement amongst the branches alerted her attention. For the fraction of a second, she believed, she had discerned the sort of flash that might be emitted by the sun glinting off a shiny-surfaced object.

"The light glancing off a field-glass, I don't doubt," grunted Barstow. "From the height of it, I would guess that our watcher is rather small of stature. About five foot five, I would hazard. He seems mightily interested in the house."

"But why would anyone want to keep watch upon this house? Why, no one even knows we are here, so far as I can tell."

The ironmaster continued to pretend he was merely gazing out of the window, but he said to Briony in an undertone, "Now, Miss Mitchem, if you will just drift out of the door, chatting with me as you go—for we don't know how much of the room can be seen—then run like the very devil to arouse the servants and enlist the aid of the Graf von Ahlden, I will keep watch."

The schoolmistress did as she was bidden, calling urgently for help the moment she was in the hallway. The count appeared almost at once, and she explained the situation.

"Wait here, if you please, miss, while I fetch my pistol." When he returned, menservants were dispatched the long way round the park to head off the intruder from that direction, while she and the count, he wearing a light cloak over his shoulder to conceal the primed firearm, sallied forth with seeming aimlessness across the lawn.

Keeping an eye toward the trees, the count tried to dissuade her from accompanying him. "There might be considerable danger, dear lady. I hesitate to expose you to such a situation."

"If you think, count," she replied with an artful laugh, "that I am going to allow you to have all the adventure, you are quite mistaken. This concerns me far more than it does you."

He smiled, but it was only camouflage for their monitor. "I am bound to say, miss, that I believe you take the whole thing much too lightly. It might well concern my ward."

Lightly she linked her arm through his free one as they slowly angled toward the thicket. "And speaking of that, sir, am I correct in believing you were unusually agitated by my request for wider spacing between your visits of inspection?"

He looked rather startled. "This seems hardly the time and place to discuss it, but I am bound to say, my dear lady, that I found the request rather impertinent. I expect I shall go on the way I have begun."

"Even at the risk of delaying the progress of the princess?" she enquired. "You must have seen that when you are present she reverts to her old clumsy self."

He shrugged. "I was merely afraid that she had made little progress at all. Do you assure me that she has changed?"

"Immeasurably."

They were near the brake and she tried to peer through the branches, but they were too thick and she could see nothing.

"I can only judge by what I behold, you see," he pointed out. "I can see that she has lost weight, of course."

Briony could take pride in that. "Her complexion is clearing as well," she mentioned, "but there is another consideration involved."

"Ah? And that is?"

"And that is, sir, that I suspect the ironmaster to be very

jealous of his daughter's honour and quite unforgiving where it is concerned. I doubt that he takes a continental view of such things."

The Graf von Ahlden did not so much as bat an eye at what he must certainly consider to be further impertinence upon the part of this young woman. Instead, he merely observed calmly, "I am, of course, happy that you have drawn my attention to this lapse on my part. I had no idea I was becoming so obvious." He took his eyes away from the thicket to rest them on her for a brief moment. "I find the working of your mind to be very interesting."

They were almost upon the thicket now, and Briony strained her ears and eyes for any telltale sign that the observer still skulked within, but the count was not prepared to play the game out in such a subtle fashion. When they were quite near the edge, he threw back the cloak and pointed the gun directly at the tangle.

"Whoever you are, if you come out with your hands above your head, you will not be harmed, but if I do not see you before I have reached the count of ten, I will open fire."

There was no answer, and, after a moment, he began to count. "One . . . two . . . three . . ."

From deeper in the park they could hear the voices of the menservants shouting back and forth to each other. With a smothered curse, the count sprang directly into the thicket, the pistol exploding as he did so. Briony shrieked in surprise, half expecting him to emerge with bloody hands, but he came back with merely an annoyed expression.

"Gone. There was definitely someone there, for the interior of the brake is quite trampled, but the miscreant made his escape by some jugglery." He held out a bit of cloth for her inspection.

"What is that?"

"Only a handkerchief. I expect he dropped it in his haste."

One of the menservants came running toward them.

"There *was* someone, miss, we found the track, but the blackguard must be devilish clever to have made such a clean escape. I can't think how he came to know the grounds so well. We'll be keeping a sharp eye out from now on, you can be sure. It reflects badly on the house, you know, that any of our guests should be placed in this position."

Briony could see the ironmaster approaching from the other direction. It appeared that he, too, had tried to head the miscreant off. She reflected that it might have proved quite dangerous to him if he had, unarmed as he was, met the man alone.

"Halloo!" he called. As he approached he explained, "I saw the little fellow leaving his hiding place, and I dashed off to intercept him, but demmed if he is not a sight more sprightly than I am." He looked at the scrap of linen she was holding. "Hello, what is that you have?"

Briony looked down at the handkerchief and saw something which had escaped her attention before. In the corner of the square was unobtrusively embroidered, white upon white, the represenation of a coronet.

$=$ **11** $=$

"I BELIEVE THAT YOU can now appreciate," said the Graf von Ahlden, "that we have undoubtedly been *less* attentive in regard to the young ladies than overprotective. In light of today's happening, I have grave doubts about their security here, though, I admit, I chose the house myself."

"I have said nothing at all about being secure, your lordship," Briony replied. "To be frank the problem has never arisen in my past experience, and, I confess, I have never even considered it. What I complained of was the effect your frequent visits were having upon the young women you and Mr. Barstow placed in my care. In the case of Miss Barstow, perhaps, the question is not so much one of time as of slow exposure to a world outside her previous experience, but for the princess . . . that is, Isabella . . . the element of time is quite crucial, or so you have led me to believe."

She had heard her error even as it fell from her lips and had moved on quickly in the hope that sheer speed might disguise the slip, but she saw from Barstow's quick glance that he had absorbed it for future reference.

"I have given the matter a bit of thought by now," he said, "and I find that I am ready to agree. I believe it is not so much a matter of safety, for we can always hire guards, if it comes to that. But if Miss Mitchem is right, it may be that the lassies will come along more quickly if you and I, count, are not so often in attendance. It is only a matter of a month, and I expect that Annie can do as well without me if she applies herself." He stroked his strongly defined jaw. "As to the other matter, we have no evidence as to who the miscreant might have been.

"I wonder if we should not have another servant, someone to patrol about at night acting as a watchman, you know. I vow I would rest more easily."

"But this incident was in the daytime," Briony protested. "For all we know it was some local lad having a bit of a gig."

"Fun is fun," the count answered, "but any real danger would come after dark, you see."

She shook her head. "I have the sense that this is all quite beside the point and that you are making far too much of it. Keep a close eye, by all means, and even hire a watchman, if it pleases you, but, I beg you, do not make the young women feel that they are confined in a prison. Who can tell what will come to pass? This all may sort itself into something perfectly simple and ordinary."

"But we do not know that, do we?" asked the count. "However, you may be right. There is, however, the question of the handkerchief. I hope you will not suggest that some young village lout carries about an eyewiper with a coronet embroidered in the corner. Even in jolly old England I shouldn't think there would be too many of those about, eh?"

But so, for the moment, they left it, though the gentlemen elected to stay the night. Subsequent events, they knew, would show whether their caution had been right or wrong.

In her dreams that night the Princess Isabella, who had been very good about the matter of diet, dreamed of a vanilla snow glacé and awoke in the darkness with a ravenous gnawing at the pit of her stomach. For a long while she lay in the warm silence thinking about it, and the more she thought the more demanding the pangs became. She dwelt upon the succulent roast which had been served at dinner, on the rich and redolent cheeses, and above all the glacé, that supreme confection of spun sugar and cream custard which she had been denied in the interest of her forthcoming nuptials. If she were in the kitchen now she would not seek that out, of course, but be quite content with simple food, a bath bun or a slice of dry brown bread, almost anything to alleviate this suffering which she recognised as more a hunger of the spirit than a physical craving. It would be useless to go to the kitchens, she told herself, for she would only do so to test her willpower. She truly loved the new form which was beginning to shape itself beneath her increasingly looser garments, but the vanilla snow glacé remained a powerful image. She knew the way to the kitchens, but to reach them one had to pass through the dark and silent house alone. She knew, of course, that the stories of trolls and dragons with which she had been frightened to sleep by her nurse were merely fantasy, but it was a very dark house. She often wished she had not led such a withdrawn life in Thoningen. If she had been more outgoing—more like Anne Barstow, for example—she might have faced the shadows with high courage, she was sure.

She tried to will herself back to sleep, but the thought of food, she found, became more compelling the harder one tried to banish it. At length she sat up in bed and swung her feet over the side. If she had not the courage of Miss Barstow, the next best thing might be to enlist her aid. They shared the deportment classes of Mr. Biddy, costume sessions with Mrs. Biddy, and the professed ideals of Miss Mitchem, but they had never become close. Although, truth to tell, Isabella had patterned some of her own physical movements upon the more attractive ones of the ironmaster's daughter.

Quietly Isabella slipped a light peignoir about her shoulders and started toward the door. She had no doubt that since supper had been hours ago, Miss Barstow might even welcome an opportunity for such an adventure. It would do no harm to ask. Creeping along the passage, she tapped discreetly upon the other young woman's door. Was it mere fancy that she could discern a faint glow of candlelight?

A whisper in return. "Who is there?"

"Isabella."

The door opened a crack as if the occupant wanted to make absolutely certain who was in the hall, then flung wider. "What is it? It must be the middle of the night."

"I saw your light and . . . and . . ." Isabella answered, fishing wildly for a plausible excuse. "I wondered if you were ill."

Anne bit her lower lip. "I couldn't sleep. Supper was not very filling, was it? I have almost been tempted to sneak belowstairs to the pantry."

"I keep dreaming of the vanilla snow glacé," Isabella confessed.

"It must be gone," Anne sighed, "but anything would do. I feel as if I have a great gaping hole where my stomach should be. Do you ever get that way?"

Isabella giggled. "I came to ask you to go there with me. I am a little nervous of the house in the dark."

Anne looked understanding of that, but she felt it necessary to ask, "What if we are caught?"

Isabella's old air of hauteur returned, and she lifted her chin. "We are guests, after all, not mere schoolgirls."

But it was rather a schoolgirl adventure to creep step by step down the long curving stair to the great hall, huddling together at every creak, shivering at every shadow. They crossed the hall and approached the lower stairs which led down to the servants' hall. Isabella paused. She recognised that beyond this point they were definitely trespassing.

"Dare we?" she asked. In reply Anne merely clutched her stomach and pantomimed a groan.

"Best put the candle out," she whispered. Silently they crept, one step at a time, down, down, down into a seeming black pit. The door at the bottom was shut, but it opened readily enough.

Anne hesitated. "Where do the servants sleep?"

"In the attics, I believe," Isabella replied softly. "All but cook and butler. They have their own chambers off the servants' hall. Just through that door, I would guess. We must tread very softly. They are the dangerous ones."

"How do you know all this?" Anne hissed.

Isabella was happy the darkness hid her blush. "When I first came, I made it my business to find out. I thought I would use the knowledge sooner than this."

Her companion understood at once. "And you have held out all this time?" she asked admiringly. "La, you *are* strong."

"Not so strong," Isabella murmured sibilantly. "I am here now, *nein?*"

For some reason, silly and pointless as it was, this sent them both into a storm of giggles, exacerbated by the need for quiet. Falling into each other's arms they buried their heads in each other's shoulders to stifle the laughter, but it was of little benefit. Anne, at last, struck out at her companion playfully.

"Here, if you cannot behave, I'll send you to your room."

"Without supper?" Isabella asked, and they were off again.

The whole episode had moved from the earlier pangs of hunger to a supreme schoolgirl silliness. The joke could only be put to rest now by the completion of what they had set out to do. The pantry had been designated as their objective, though, somehow, it no longer mattered whether they found food there or not. The mere stealing of provisions no longer had any meaning other than a part of this arcane rite of passage.

Carefully they crept past the dining hall, looking fearfully beyond the door of the cook's room. The kitchen was flooded with the moonlight that fell through the tall, uncurtained windows.

"Where is the pantry?" Anne asked. In reply Isabella merely pointed across the large room to the two doors in the far wall. One, she guessed, led to the scullery; the other to the pantry, although she was not certain which was which. She had, after all, never been here at night. It rather changed things about. Huddled together in the shadows, they gathered the last of their energies together for the final assault when, with a faint squeak, one of the doors across the room began slowly to open.

Isabella clapped her hand over her mouth to stifle the little squeal of surprise that came unbidden to her lips; Anne clung to her companion with a grip of steel, leaving bruises which were not discovered until morning. As they watched, petrified in their places, the pantry door slowly edged open, and a slender figure, laden down with food-stuffs, emerged.

Gott in Himmel, thought Isabella, *she has a hunger worse than mine*. Anne merely started in surprise and relaxed her grip somewhat when she saw that the burglar was slighter of stature than herself, for the girl was only of medium height, slim, and, as they could see when she moved into the beams of moonlight, of an extraordinary dark pretti-ness. In her two hands she carried a silver tray upon which there were enough provisions to feed a more moderate eater for a week. She set it very carefully down upon the table, then returned to the pantry. When she came back she held a pickle-jar, which she put with the rest before she crossed to the dresser for a cup and plate. Then, with precise exactitude, she laid out a place at table: plate, dish upon it, knives and spoons to the right, forks to the left. It was obvious from the number of utensils she found necessary that she was gently raised. Now she cut a slice of the cold roast, added a bit of cheese, and speared a pickle to add piquancy. A slice of bread, cut rather thickly, spread with butter in equal proportion, and, into the cup with which she furnished herself, she poured refreshment from the china milk jug.

Oddly enough, all this preparation rather took the edge off the watchers' hunger. Silently clinging to each other in the shadows, they watched with amazement as this slim young creature downed a meal substantial enough for a navvy. The burglar was too engrossed in her repast to notice them at first, but as she chewed and looked about. Inevitably, her eyes fell upon them, shadowy though they were. Carefully she swallowed, then cleared her throat.

"Pardon me," she whispered. "Is someone there?"

Both of the older young women sighed in relief. "Yes," whispered the ironmaster's daughter. She stepped forward and Isabella followed.

"Are you really going to eat all of that?" the princess whispered.

The girl assented in a matter-of-fact manner. "You cannot imagine how hungry one gets," she confided. Then, remembering her manners, she asked, "Would you care for some?"

Suddenly, for both, the ravening hunger returned. "But it is too dangerous here," Anne sensibly observed. "If we carry it all upstairs, we can feast in private. I am afraid cook is formidable, and, if we are caught, there will be a terrible to-do."

So everything was carefully loaded on the tray again. With the addition of additional plates and cups it was quite heavy, and Anne took one handle while the intruder took the other. It was odd, the ironmaster's daughter observed to herself, that she should so readily accept a complete stranger who had obviously broken into the house, as a sort of comrade-in-arms in such peculiar circumstances. Especially after the hubble-bubble of this afternoon's excitement.

Isabella led the way, opening doors and padding along quietly in her bare feet. Sneaking carefully through the servants' hall, they fancied they heard a sound behind the private chamber of cook and butler and froze in the middle of the room. The sound came again but they recognised that it was domestic, not an alarum. Nevertheless they skittered up the steps and hurried across the wide and polished expanse of the great hall toward the stairway, half dissolved in laughter and half terrified of detection.

But bare feet do not afford purchase upon smooth floors, and Isabella felt herself slipping as they went. She strove to right herself but it was of no avail. She slid for a foot, then fell. Reaching blindly out for support, she caught at Anne's arm; but Anne was helping to carry the tray of food. She swayed, trying to keep her own balance, and, in doing so, disturbed that of the girlish burglar.

"*Dios!*" The slim figure danced, trying to hold the tray at a level and herself as well. Anne, reaching out to be of aid, made it worse by striking the little stack of china cups a glancing blow. There was a crash of crockery, an echo through the hall, and then, for a long moment afterward, there was silence.

It did not last long. Within moments there were lights appearing from all directions. The butler, with his candlestick, came hurrying up the steps from belowstairs. Briony appeared upon the landing in decorous deshabille, a china lamp in her hand. From along the bedroom corridor came both of the visiting gentlemen, bedsheets clutched about their middles; the Graf von Ahlden with his pistol in hand and the ironmaster with the firetongs, which, though out of use for the summer, still reposed beside his bedroom fireplace. They all slowly converged upon the embarrassed young women. Pushing past the gentlemen in their imitation togas, Briony held her light high above the head of the young female intruder.

"Why, Consuela Ferreblanco, what on earth are you doing here?"

= 12 =

CONSUELA PUSHED THE empty platter away at last. Upon it rested only the gnawed bone of the roast, the denuded stems of a grape cluster, and a few crumbs of the loaf which she had single-handedly put away. Though the other young women had eaten a few scraps of the provisions stolen from the larder, she had accounted for most of the feast while Anne and Isabella looked guiltily on.

The dining room was far from empty. It was aglow with candles, and the Hollymead butler hovered unobtrusively in the background, waiting to be of service, but also as interested as any in the company in the tale the young runaway had to tell. He reflected happily that never since he and cook had come to Hollymead had there been such diversion as that provided by Miss Mitchem and her company. It was better than a theatre piece and equally satisfying, for he and his wife found themselves not to be on the outside looking on, but drawn well within the parameters of the drama. He rather fancied, in fact, that he had once seen someone very like that Mr. Biddy on the boards at some time in the past, though cook pooh-poohed such a notion.

"What, that gangling beanpole on the stage? Who'd pay to see him, I wonder?" Nevertheless the butler had his recollection and paid smartly for it, too, he remembered.

Today, of course, had been the capper of all; he could hardly hope for better. The former tenants he had served had all been stiff and formal, as grandly impressed with their own state as living amongst the magnificences of Hollymead, but with this lot, a new sense of life had come along. The splendid beginning of this afternoon's chase and the threat of danger had been followed by this midnight adventure with the young ladies running about in wrappers and bare feet, a pretty little burglar raiding the pantry (and wouldn't cook be that upset?), and a great hurrying and scurrying about. The other servants had come trooping down from their beds in the attics, of course, but he had packed them off again, quick as mice, with a bit of censure against spying on their betters. Which, of course, was exactly just what he himself was doing. He didn't mind it in the least. Do as I say, not as I do.

The gentlemen had been a treat, had they not? Not half! Although now suitably dressed in shirts and breeches, they had looked proper guys, they had, all garbed in sheets and waving firearms and pokers about in such a reckless manner. Even handsome young Mr. Redmond had latterly appeared in nightshirt and robe, much surprised to see the newcomer.

"Miss Ferreblanco, is that you? I thought you were sailing off to Cuba?"

Well might he have asked, for to the butler's eye, she had the very appearance of a saucy lad. Young Redmond could appreciate, as the butler could not, how great an alteration there had been in Consuela since she had bid such a tearful good-bye to his sister on Prize Day. But even the butler could appreciate that a laborer's coarsely woven smock with breeches and boots were not her customary attire.

"All your lovely hair," Briony mourned, ruffling what was left of it, an unruly brown mop.

"I had to cut it, you see, madame," Consuela explained rather defensively. "I expect that my papa will be much overwrought, but I could not be a self-respecting boy with locks to my waist, you know."

"I daresay you have had a frightening time," said Redmond in an admiring tone of voice.

Consuela rolled her eyes, but they sparkled mischievously as well. "Actually, it has been rather a treat," she said in English schoolgirl idiom, "though, *por Dios*, I have no idea what measures Papa will take when he finds I have slipped away from poor Señora Emilia, who has travelled so far to accompany me home."

Isabella, who was most definitely of two minds concerning her own nuptials to a man she had never seen, much less grown to love, pressed for details. "Where was it your intention to go?"

Consuela wiped her mouth delicately and shrugged. "It did not seem to matter. I was about to board the ship with Señora Emilia when she told me that Don Pepe was in Europe and would be returning on the same vessel. I did not think, you see; I only ran, ran, ran."

"Were you afraid to meet him?" asked Isabella. "Were you afraid he might reject you?" she continued, thereby revealing her own secret fears. She stole a rather jealous look at Redmond, as well, since it seemed to her he was paying a great deal of enthusiastic attention to this pretty adventuress. Before meeting Redmond, Isabella had never had a friend of the opposite sex, and she felt a little possessive of him—which would undoubtedly have alarmed Redmond had he known.

Consuela, for her part, merely looked at the princess blankly. "Reject? Oh, how happy I would be, señorita, if only he could be persuaded to do that! It is an arranged marriage, you see, with a friend of my father; a man whom I have never met." She sipped the last of her tea and looked mightily unconcerned.

Briony remonstrated with her gently. "But you cannot keep running forever, my dear child."

"No," Consuela agreed, "I expect I shall have to go home at last, but I could not face it so soon. I slipped away from my duenna and ran back to you, Miss Mitchem. I somehow thought you could make it right."

"But how did you find your way to Hollymead?"

Consuela smiled. "If you can credit it, madame, Mrs. Travers directed me. When I remember what a dragon I always thought her when I was at school, I am quite ashamed. No one could have been kinder than your cook. She fed me, she loaned me a bit of money—more than she could easily spare, I expect, and she set me on the right road to find you again."

"But how did you come by the clothes?" Redmond probed, and Consuela laughed merrily.

"Do you not recognise them, sir? They are your own. I expect if you look closely you will see the paint on the hem of this smock." She flirted her eyes, but he did not take her up on the suggestion, and the ironmaster soon claimed her attention.

"A young slip of a thing like you alone and about the country?" asked Barstow. "You took life lightly, my lassie. Who knows what could have happened before you found Miss Mitchem again?" The ironmaster looked worriedly at his daughter as if he feared that she too might take it into her head to embark upon such a daft adventure.

Briony stood up, carefully drawing her peignoir about her. "Well, I shall keep you safely by me and send a letter off to your father in the morning, though heaven knows how long it will take to arrive in Cuba. I suppose we had also better send word to your friend Mrs. Travers, saying that you have arrived without mishap, eh? As for your clothing, we shall have to fit you out from the other young ladies until Mrs. Biddy can make up some frocks and gowns. I expect that all you have with you is the costume you are wearing.

"Except, of course," she added with a light laugh, "the handkerchief you dropped in the thicket."

Consuela frowned, obviously perplexed. "Thicket, madame?"

"Yes, the little copse of trees at the edge of the lawn from where you watched the house with your glass today."

"No, madame, I watched the house from the far side of

the drive until all the lights had gone out, and even then I waited for a long time before I dared creep inside."

Briony smiled understandingly. "No, my dear, I do not mean this evening, but this afternoon when you so foolishly ran away, leaving your pretty coroneted handkerchief behind as a telltale."

The Cuban girl blinked. "I do assure you, madame, that you are much mistaken. I have never run away in my life, and, if I had come to the house during the day, I should have presented myself at once. It was only my"—she spread her hands helplessly—"my outlandish appearance which prevented me from doing so this evening. I feared you might take me for a blackguard or a housebreaker."

"Which, in fact, you were, I believe?" commented the Graf von Ahlden, but his eyes worriedly sought those of Benjamin Barstow, even as the others laughed at his sally.

Lying awake in the darkness after Consuela had been found a bed and the others had returned to sleep, ironmaster Barstow found himself in something of a quandary. Ever since he had first begun to stray forth from his snug house beneath Bloodybush Edge in the Cheviot Hills, he had—sometimes more, sometimes less—been increasingly conscious of a stirring within himself to reach upward, to go beyond the narrow limits to which his birth and occupation might ordinarily have bound him. It had been the one factor above all others that had driven him to succeed, to achieve what his fellows had or could not.

In furthering his daughter he had, in a sense, really been furthering himself, he recognised. Through her, a sort of extension of himself, he had been striving for something greater than his own experience, had been seeking to break out of his protective prison of class and background to explore the great world he sensed lay beyond.

In all of this, he was aware that certain dangers lay. His daughter, for example, must eventually be cleaving to another man, must be seeking a home and hearth of her own, not his. Barstow was aware, being no one's fool, that by this thrusting forward of Anne, he risked losing her altogether. Not a great risk, certainly, but a present one. He had seen, for example, how appreciatively the Graf von Ahlden had allowed his eyes to rest on her, and, if such a high-born gentleman might do so, then others would surely follow. Ben Barstow was also not so foolish as to deny that this was but the natural course of life, but it gave him pause. The changes which had come about in Anne, during even this scant month, were eye-opening. The lass had been like some tiny, furled flowerbud which was now beginning to open into the glory of full blossom. It was a gratifying thing to watch, the more so that this day, to his own amazement, Benjamin Barstow had found himself beginning to feel certain similar stirrings within himself.

The ironmaster had long since accustomed himself to the idea that he would, sooner or later, find himself alone. It was not a pleasant prospect, for he was a companionable man. The most poignant effect of the loss of his wife had been the terrible silences after she had gone. As Annie had grown, she had done much to alleviate the lack, but something in him required more. The plain fact was that ironmaster Barstow needed a wife. The unfortunate part of this important realisation was one which has afflicted peasants and knights for centuries: the lover looks always upward toward the unattainable ideal. The ironmaster had no illusions about himself; he was a plain man who had fallen fairly beneath the spell of a woman he considered quite extraordinary.

Since his first meeting with Briony Mitchem he had been unreservedly drawn to her. Nay, even before that, when Mayor Dedham of Hadrian's Green had recounted her struggle and her triumph over an adverse heritage, Barstow had felt a thrill of admiration. It had grown within him, upon meeting after meeting, but it both chagrined and dourly amused him that the young headmistress was of the certain belief that his frequent visits to Hollymead were for the sake of his daughter alone. He was amused, as well, at his own reactions in this for, without ever having spoken frankly, he had believed his feelings were clear, though not a stated intention of any sort. God knows, he had followed her about from spot to spot like a motherless puppy; undoubtedly underfoot, but believing that he thereby demonstrated his devotion.

He now laughed out loud in the darkness at the rare folly in so misleading himself. When all was done, he still had no notion whether she inclined to him or no. Certainly, he was almost of an age to be her father, but to balance that, he was hale and healthy. She sprang from landed gentry, he was aware, and had a family history longer than her arm, but his new-minted money had all the exuberance of youth with no clinging melancholy attached to it. He had been told the story of her parents and their obsession, and he guessed it might be saddening for her to look backward. He himself took no great joy in doing so. No, no, the future was all ahead.

He shared with von Ahlden, though, the nagging uncertainty as to the safety of this place for the young women. Had it been left to him, there would be, as of today, a constant patrol of borderwalkers at the Hollymead boundaries, day and night. He still felt a nagging annoyance that von Ahlden had allowed Miss Mitchem to walk out with him across the lawn to flush the covert. Granted, it had been empty of all save the handkerchief, (he himself had tracked the intruder for a space), but it might not have been. The count might have been exposing the young woman to unknown dangers.

But, he now surmised, if danger existed, it centered not upon Miss Mitchem or his daughter, but the other lass— the stout one, as he still thought of her, although it was no longer strictly true. The princess, he supposed he might dub her in his mind, if the tongueslip the headmistress had made was strictly accurate.

And, thinking of this princess, if such she truly was—he

was not yet completely convinced of it—what great mystery surrounded her that she should be sent to school in England (and for such a short time), and who was she that her security should be threatened? Was there some real danger which menaced her and left von Ahlden in such a sweat when the little kerchief was found?

And, for that matter, what *of* that little scrap of linen with its inconspicuous coronet? To whom had it belonged, if not to the little Spanish wench? And—if it was not the girl—who was it who had so inquisitively trained his field glass upon Hollymead House? Someone rather small for a man, average for a girl, or a slightly built lad. Who was it who . . . ? Why was it that his thoughts always began to wander just when he reached an interesting avenue of inquiry? Strange how they sometimes jumbled all together.

Who was it that . . . ?

And the ironmaster slept.

= 13 =

THE CABINET ROOM in Schulenberg Palace held treasure of all ages as testimonial to the wide-ranging interests of the previous ruler, an inveterate collector. On one wall was a tapestry in brave red, blues, and golds, depicting the victory of Ostro in 1322; against a further wall, beneath the high-set windows, was a splendid inlaid cabinet of some close-grained wood, now darkened with age to the shade of ebony, but set with tortoise shell and silver. The oaken panels of the walls were painted green with a handsome design picked out in gold leaf, and above the massive chair at the far end of the table—the only chair with cushions and padded arms—were the bear and unicorn of Bratslau, carved and gilded, supporting between them the shield of the Duke of Berengaria.

The square-shouldered gentleman who now occupied the chair was not the duke himself, nor even his appointed representative, but one who had, from time to time in the past, acted as regent in time of need. At first look one might say, "This jolly-featured but commonplace man is sitting as the head of the council as a lark, a sort of jest allowed by the others only until the true master appears upon the scene." But, with a closer view, you might alter your opinion. Although his cheeks were round and glossy as a sweet birtle, his limbs were hard; although his smile was wide and cheerful, his eyes were as penetrating as tempered steel; and, though at that first glance he had seemed to be an amiable fellow, there was, behind the diplomatic mask he wore, a sternness of purpose. This was the political genius Mansdorf, who, as Metternich's good right hand, had been the true architect of the German Confederation at the Congress of Vienna, though few recognised the point. It was he, moreover, who had chivvied the council into recognition of young Rudolph as heir to the throne of Berengaria, despite certain reservations on his own part.

He had not, however, been of the faction of the diet which pressed for a closer relation with Schleswig-Holstein-Gundorp-Thoningen through intermarriage. He had his reasons for this policy, though they were not ones which he could easily disclose to that august assembly. He had chosen, instead, to speak to only a few, here in the council chamber rather than the *diet halle*. The statement he had just made in defense of his policy left the remainder of the council stunned.

"Are you seriously alleging, Graf von Mansdorf, that Princess Isabella is an unfit bride for the duke?"

Mansdorf beamed upon his questioner. "Not in a moral sense, my dear Herr Volkert. Not, at least, in any sense which reflects upon the morals of the young woman herself. I refer only to certain irregularities in her family tree."

Volkert gave a sigh of relief. "Oh, the madness of the Wittelsbachs? I was worried there for a moment. We all know of that, my friend, it is common knowledge. But surely her mother's family has no taint of that sort, eh? And so far as we know, the Wittelsbach curse passes through the male line."

"Nevertheless," Mansdorf smiled, "the young woman could easily be a *carrier* of the Wittelsbach weakness. I say *could*, for I have become aware of a circumstance which may alter much. There has recently come to my attention a certain paper—and I see no reason to believe it is not genuine—which suggests that our stout little princess may not, in fact, be a Wittelsbach at all!"

There was a stony quietness as if he had committed the most dreadful *lèse-majesté* ever pronounced. Count

Bernhard was the first to break the silence. He leaned forward in his chair, his handsome, rather intimidating old head thrust out inquisitorially from his shoulders. "I wonder, my dear Mansdorf, if you know that I myself am connected by marriage to the Wittelsbachs?"

"Of course! Of course, I do, my friend, but I am speaking dynastically, not personally. I am labouring under the belief that we are all loyal Berengarians here, concerned with national honour. In the long run, I feel it is always cleverest not to be clever at all, but to lay one's cards frankly on the table from the start."

He fairly emanated bonhomie, but his listeners were old acquaintances who knew very well that behind the facade was a brain as cold and clicking as any mechanical device yet invented. "What I am about to disclose, in any case, reflects not in the least upon Wittelsbach blood, for, in my humble opinion, Wittelsbach blood does not enter into the question."

"Do you mean to imply, sir, that the Princess Isabella is not all she should be in the matter of legitimacy?" asked Herr Huber, standing as he spoke, which none of the others had done. "Well, there have been mésalliances in the past and no one the worse for them. Brought in fresh blood, in fact. The girl is an attested virgin, is she not, and politically proper enough?"

"I would be happier," said Mansdorf, "if she were the offspring of a steward or a stableman, than what I believe is the sad case. There could then be no foreign repercussions, only local ones, which can always be squelched easily enough."

Councillor Volkert's face took on a gravely questioning look. He listened, but it was as if he attended most closely to an undercurrent in Mansdorf's voice and not his words alone. They had been intimates as boys, these two, and knew each other well, though it had been years since they had been on the same side in any question. Why, then, he wondered, had *he* been brought to this congression of toadies and self-servers? In looking around the table he observed now that every other man there had a reputation as a vacillator, able to turn his coat where it seemed most profitable to himself or to whatever cause he espoused. Fairly speaking, each one here *did* follow some cause or other, even though it usually served himself as much as he served it. Each had taken a public issue and ridden it the way a child rides a hobbyhorse, obsessively, with eyes looking neither to the left or right.

Volkert's thin lips curved into a faintly self-derisive smile, and his eyebrows involuntarily lifted. Was he, too, then, considered to be a man such as these, ready to seek his own advantage by acting in concord with whichever strongman would offer him some advance? It was, verily, a notion of his character he had not previously entertained.

"Let us cut straight through to the bone, Graf von Mansdorf," he suggested, raising his voice just enough to carry over the murmuring of the sycophants. "Do I understand you to be suggesting that Princess Isabella of Thoningen is not the daughter of her purported father, but a bastard? Do you suggest, sir, that her mother was false or that the baby was smuggled in in a warming-pan?"

Mansdorf's countenance was, if anything, more benevolent beneath this raillery than it had been before. He made a show of peering around the table as Volkert had done, then said warmly, "I believe we are all friends here." He smiled more broadly, as if sharing a jest. "Or we are, at least, not avowed enemies."

There was a ripple of appreciation at this sally, and he waited for it to subside before he continued. His answer to Volkert was short and to the point, a single word in effect: "Yes."

It produced a most gratifying chorus of gasps, and he went on to further amplify it. "What I am about to tell you must never pass beyond the confines of this room, is that clear, is that agreed?" Satisfied, he went on.

"How many of you remember a physician very dear to

the heart of every sickly widow of the last generation, a man named Foss who, through sedulous flattery and benign diagnosis, amassed a small fortune and a great reputation?"

A few fingers were raised; a few nods of assent, Volkert among them.

"I know that to many he seemed a mere opportunist," Mansdorf went on, "feeding his coffers upon the gullibility of the unwary, but, I do assure you, beneath that soft and doughy exterior lurked an astute man of the world, a man of science who very well, as the peasants say, knew his noodle."

An appreciative smile went through his audience. All political considerations aside, they were fond of this engaging rascal. He might be a little too clever to be trusted completely, but he could make them laugh, and that said a great deal for him, did it not? A man who can make you laugh cannot be all bad through and through. Volkert, alert to the possibility of a game of hide-the-pea, merely waited.

"Well, my friends, the old man is quite dead now, and beyond our judgement, but he had a son, who is very much alive, and a gentleman of great curiosity. This fellow, Hans Foss, by name, came to me recently with an item of great interest which he had discovered while going over his father's possessions. It was a rather shabbily bound book filled with poorly formed scribbles, which he asked me to examine with particular attention to one specific entry and the related ones which followed. He then suggested to me that this information might be of some financial value to someone in a high place. He did not specify who.

"The book, gentlemen, as many of you will have guessed, was his casebook, a journal old Foss kept for his own purposes in which he had annotated some very curious things concerning the minutiae of his profession. The portion which young Foss called to my attention proved greatly disturbing to me. I do not wish to go into the distasteful medical specifics of the matter, but the conclusion drawn by the good doctor was that, resulting from the effects of that virulent epidemic which swept our region some years ago, Duke Ernst of Schleswig-Holstein-Gundorp-Thoningen could not have fathered a daughter— could not, in fact, have fathered a mouse, if you take my meaning."

Volkert's voice cut through. "Do you mean to say, sir, that the duke was impotent?"

"I mean to say, sir, that as a result of disease the duke was undoubtedly sterile and, if so incapacitated, could hardly have fathered the Princess Isabella."

"May I remind you, count, that Duke Ernst was widely celebrated for the number and variety of his bastards? That scarcely suggests sterility."

"Look at them, if you will, my good Volkert. Look at their birthdates. I have the list of all the known ones here, in fact, for your perusal. All born before the epidemic! All before the duke came down with his famous case of mumps!"

The list was passed around the table, barely glanced at by most, but carefully examined by Volkert and by Herr Huber.

"And so, of course, under Salic law, when dear Duke Ernst passed on, so did the crown. The present duke, as you all know, is a first cousin once removed and with certain dynastic ambitions of his own. He is as yet unmarried, but the duchess, Ernst's widow, is now a nobody. When Duke Ernst died, the princess, poor thing, was stuck away in a belowstairs closet with nothing to do but eat."

That this was quite the broadest of exaggerations was understood, but in essence it was true. Isabella was essentially as much a nobody as her mother. It would be of some prestige to the new duke that his niece should be married to the pivotal figure of the new confederation, but it could hardly count for much in the long run. The proposed alliance of the two houses, then, had astonished many.

Isabella, of a certainty, was important to Mansdorf only

because she was an obstruction to some plan of his own. And, since she was devoid of personal importance, and, since he was making such a pother of it, Volkert thought, it could only be because the count believed her to be the natural daughter of some other great figure who might, at some future time, take it into his head to meddle in the affairs of Berengaria on behalf of his offspring. It seemed now to Volkert that this was perhaps why Isabella had been chosen by Mandorf's opposition, in the hope that some great personage might be encouraged to stand as protector. And if so, if that was indeed the kernel of the case, there was only one prominent and influential person who it might logically be.

He strove to recall whether the Crown Prince of England, (now that nation's Prince Regent) had paid a visit to his other homeland, Hanover, at the time in question. And if he had, at that time, paid anything like a cousinly call upon his neighbour the incapacitated Duke of Schleswig-Holstein-Gundorp-Thoningen?

=14=

IT MUST NOT be supposed that, as the young ladies continued their elegant education, the lessons became easier. In
fact, quite the reverse was true. The more they had
achieved, the more was expected of them. Isabella was
slowly changing physically, but for Anne Barstow, the
striving seemed never to have an end. Mr. Biddy had
become something of a friend, and their confidence in him
was very great, but he never ceased to be a taskmaster and
kept them at exercises, recitations, and repetitions for hour
upon hour. He asked them to do nothing he himself could
not, but it seemed to them that there was nothing of which
he was not the master, whether it be a dance step or the
way a fan is flirted to convey a lady's intent. It sometimes
seemed to the ironmaster's daughter that her tongue grew
thick and clumsy in her mouth whenever she thought of
forming her words in the genteel fashion he demanded, but
she recognised as well that it was not for herself alone that
she must achieve. Her father looked to her, she knew, for
more than she could yet hope for.

To speak truly, she was not always altogether sure *what* it
was her father wanted, hoped, or expected of her. However
much she loved him (and it was with a devotion she could
not have expressed to him, nor would he have understood),
he had always been a man past her fathoming. Left to
herself, she might never have blossomed, yet she might
have been as happy and content as any other woman in that

harsh country from which she sprang; married by now, probably, and beginning to offer Benjamin Barstow grandchildren, turning him into the patriarch nature had very likely intended him to be. But her father had ambitions beyond that. He wanted more both for himself and for her; this very intensive education was evidence of it.

She submitted (for there could be no other word for it) to the rigours devised by Mr. Biddy, and she did it with grace and good will. She allowed herself, on the wish of her father, to be entirely given over to this regimen. There were, in fact, a few parts of the schedule which she enjoyed. Though she would never have the unerring sense of Mrs. Biddy for clothing construction, for cut and line, she learned the basic rules of dress and fashion, and her eyes were opened to considerations she had never previously encountered. Since, in the north, she had had very little knowledge of what was *comme il faut*, she had merely accepted what others, rarely more educated than herself, told her was correct. Now she even began to understand that subtle dictum which says "fashionable" and "correct" are not necessarily synonymous conceptions.

Far more difficult for her were the endless vocal exercises under Mr. Biddy's guidance and the drills in manner and deportment from Miss Mitchem. It went on and on without letup. She had not even Isabella's recreation with Redmond in the tennis court to alleviate her forced concentration.

And then, one morning, it all changed.

She had been running through the repetitious exercises, her tongue shaping the words, it seemed, in much the same way it had always done; with Mr. Biddy correcting and sighing, Mrs. Biddy, across the room, placidly sewing and smiling encouragement. From the lawn outside, she could hear the comradely laughter as Redmond and Isabella made their way to the court. It seemed a fine day out there. The air and scent drifting through the curtains, the look of the light on the grass, all called alluringly and, suddenly, she felt she could take no more; her absorption had been completed.

"I have had enough," she said, and oddly, it did not even sound like herself saying it. All sounds, she supposed, become meaningless after enough repetition. But she became slowly aware that Biddy was regarding her sharply and that Mrs. Biddy was smiling as if some personal satisfaction had overcome her.

"What did you say?" asked the man.

She made a graceful, but despairing gesture. "Oh, sir, it will never change. I go over and over the same words, the same phrases day after day, and it seems that I will be saying them in the same way forever." She lifted her chin a little in defiance. "It is finished."

"Say it again, please," he requested, and, thinking he was making a mockery, tears sprang to her eyes.

"It is finished, I tell you! I cannot do more!"

Shockingly, he began to laugh. "Can you hear yourself?" he asked. "Can you hear what you are saying?"

Anne frowned, her feelings hurt. She had said nothing out of the ordinary. But she understood that something *had* changed. She listened in her mind to the words she had most recently spoken and even they seemed slightly different, though she could not have said how. Across the room, Mrs. Biddy put the final touches on a new ball dress, a frock of tulle over a rose-coloured slip of satin.

"You've done it," she said. "Can't you hear? I can."

"I have no idea what you are talking about, either of you!" Anne almost was tempted to stamp her foot.

" 'Eye-ther'?" asked Mr. Biddy. "Not 'eather'? 'Idea,' not 'notion'?"

His extreme archness annoyed her exceedingly. "What are you suggesting, Mr. Biddy? I cannot think why you are making such sport of me."

But something had ticked in her head, and she began to hear herself quite differently. She understood that what Mr. Biddy had been teaching her was not a slavish imitation of the upper classes, but something far better. It was not speaking that was important; it was listening.

"Do you hear her, mother?" Biddy asked his wife. "She has it at last. She has found her ear!"

The moment was a revelation to her. She could now say what she liked; more than that—what she intended! For now she could hear the difference. She could use her speech, her voice, her brain to achieve the effect her ideas required at any time. Yes, the voice as well. Now that she had found her ear, now that she could *hear*, she could place her voice where it most pleasingly fell. Her face became suffused with an intense delight as she understood just what had come about.

Of course her education was not finished, no matter what she had proclaimed. It had, in fact, only begun. By Anne's own wish nothing was mentioned to Miss Mitchem, nor to the tennis players, Redmond and Isabella. Let the others realise it as she had done.

Now she was fired with a second wind of enthusiasm. Everything must be fitted into place. Manners must be perfected, costuming must be understood and selected. Her mind must broaden itself, she knew, so that she could move unconsciously in the great world into which she was about to enter; *she* must do it, no one else could do it for her. It was a great challenge, a new way of thinking, of perception . . . and it was, oh, very exciting!

Briony, when she began to understand what had come about (for Biddy never drew it to her attention) resolved to now place the girl in situations and places where she could exercise her newfound abilities, honing and polishing them. It was given to Anne, at teatime, to have to pour and serve; at luncheon she was requested to preside over the table when Miss Mitchem found it convenient to be absent; she was even, of an evening, asked to favour them with some air from the border where she had spent her childhood, and it was this, above all, that demonstrated how far she had come, for the voice, while scarcely of professional quality, was sweet. The peacock scream had vanished forever.

The changes in Anne Barstow changed her view of life as well. Within days she assumed a new confidence; she was no longer awkward from shyness as she had been wont to be. Her father sensed it only slowly, but the Graf von Ahlden watched with great appreciation as she began to blossom. Each time he came to visit Hollymead the girl had matured further. Mindful of Miss Mitchem's discreet warning concerning the propriety of his attentions, the count made it a point never to be alone with Miss Barstow, but his behaviour in public was beyond the scope of such prohibitions. He deferred to her, complimented her, praised her to her father, and even once or twice took the great liberty of suggesting some correction of social usage.

A matter of cutting fish served whole set the seal upon the direction of his regard.

It was at a supper under the trees on a soft evening. The cook had racked her brain for an appropriate dish and was saved at the last minute by the boy who arrived with a dozen of the prettiest, sleekest silverbacks that ever were seen. Too fine they were and too fragile to serve them in any other way but beautifully poached and presented upon a bed of cress. When they were brought across the lawn to the table they were greeted with sighs and cries of delight—by all but Anne Barstow. The expression of the fish eye staring up at her from the plate was more than she was prepared to face. She looked down at it, away, back again with a flushed face and a frantic expression. It was not that she did not like fish, she did, but she looked at this one with incomprehension. She knew it was to be eaten, but she had not the slightest clew as to how she should do so. Miss Mitchem was at the head of the table, but both she and Isabella were out of the line of sight. And, perversely, Anne did not wish to have to ask. She must someday step off on her own and the moment seemed upon her.

Another foot beneath the table bumped against hers, but she was too concerned with her problem to notice. She looked to see how her father had chosen to manage, but it was obvious that his attack was a most impractical one, and he was confronted by a plethora of small bones as a result. The nudge or bump came against her foot again, almost as if the count opposite her were deliberately treading upon her toe. When she took time to look up from her plate, he gave her a strongly significant look. She had been aware for some days that his interest in her was growing, but she hoped he was not proposing to begin some campaign of subtle molestation, for she really did not feel at the moment much inclined toward polite dalliance. Now, however, his eyes grew very wide, the pupils themselves seeming to enlarge and grow darker. He looked very pointedly at her plate, then down at his own. Now, as she watched, he took up the knife with the oddly curved blade and carefully sliced off the head of his silverback and placed it in a small dish to the side. Looking at her, he waited. Anne did the same, banishing the fish eye as quickly as she could.

Now the count made a shallow incision, end to end, in the body of the fish, slicing just under the skin and opening it up flat. She again followed his lead and continued to do so when he cut underneath the backbone with the knife's sharp, curved point and with the aid of the fish fork lifted the skeleton whole to join the discarded head. This done, the pair cut the remainder of their respective fishes into small bits and ate them very daintily indeed, beaming at each other all the while. Perhaps only Redmond of all those at table was unaware that something very serious had happened between them.

It did not in the least outrage Benjamin Barstow, but it puzzled him mightily. He found that recently he was puzzled by a great many things and one of them was that his lass Annie had metamorphosed into a completely unknown creature; into a something that even he could recognise as the beginnings of a very great lady. Her very bearing had altered within the past fortnight, and her voice, which he had always found a little regrettable, having been raised with the gentle modulations of border women, seemed of a sudden to have become a new thing entirely, distinctly hers, but fuller of body and far sweeter of tone. It came to him that, whatever it was he had expected, the educational processes of Miss Mitchem had been worth every farthing. All of this so surprised him that, out of a decent regard for his own intelligence and a certain sense of fairness, he looked, as well, along the table toward Isabella Wittelsbach and perceived that she was "the stout one" of his memory no more. Sturdy she would doubtless always be, even, in her own time, an imposing figure of a woman, but now he saw a young girl transformed by something as strong as that which had changed Anne. Following the direction of her eyes, he saw that they rested on the handsome young devil of an artist who had been Miss Mitchem's reason, he understood, for engaging in this experiment in the beginning.

Princess Isabella was neither so besotted nor so secure that she dared gaze uninterruptedly at the object of her infatuation, but, when she did so, it was with a deference and regard that made it easy enough to read her mind. It was a situation, Ben suspected, that might lead to a pretty mess. But, then, looking at Briony Mitchem, he revised his opinion. She knew exactly what was happening in all cases, of that he was sure. Again his regard of her was raised, not in a romantic fashion, but in justified admiration of her certain capabilities. She put him in mind of the women of the borderland—quiet, calm, and very much in control of their own destinies.

= 15 =

THE WATCHER IN the shadows abandoned the thicket and moved stealthily across the lawn toward Hollymead House. The guard and his dogs, posted through the instructions of Barstow and von Ahlden, had made his patrol through this part of the grounds and passed on to the orchard edge of the property, thinking far less about intruders than of the supper ahead and the contents of the forbidden jug with which he expected to wash it down and warm the watches of the night.

It was a dazzlingly clear, though moonless, night, and the starshine was sufficient to light the intruder's way to the house. He had spent enough time here by now to know exactly where he was going. Questions had been raised by him employers as to the exact relationship between the Princess Isabella and the handsome young Redmond Mitchem. So far he had been able to prove nothing, which had served to annoy his masters. He had tried to explain to them that habitual companionship in the tennis court was no guarantee of light behaviour after dark, but so eager were they for any evidence whatsoever that might discredit the alliance of Berengaria with Schleswig-Holstein-Gundorp-Thoningen that they refused to believe his attestations to the contrary. However true it might be, though, that Isabella sighed for the young man, there was no indication that it had gone further. It was much more likely, the watcher personally believed, that the youth might be seduced by that extremely light-minded young

Caribbean girl, with her flashing eyes and saucy ways. She would, in any case, have been the watcher's choice, had he been given a choice. But as for the boy seducing Isabella, no. It seemed unlikely that the thought had even occurred to Redmond—and the princess slimming nicely down to a pleasant armful, too. Quietly, the watcher let himself into the house by one of the many entrances he had discovered. In huge old piles such as this one, the very idea of keeping out a professional like himself was a matter for hilarity.

Briony had come down early after a restless night. Something had awakened her in the small hours, and all the alarums concerning the safety of the house had kept her not awake, but in that annoying half-world between waking and sleeping. That world is populated with unseen spectres and vastly disturbing shadows which vanish in the morning, but leave you exhausted by the activities of your own imagination. She had been certain, for instance, that she had detected a series of padded footfalls in the corridor outside her chamber. That had been mere foolishness, of course. She had even gone so far as to light her candle and creep out to investigate. There had been no one, as she knew would be the case, but some part of her mind would not accept that, and she had tossed restlessly, scolding herself and making vain promises to herself about how quickly she was going to sink into the waiting arms of Morpheus. It was to no avail.

Surprisingly, she felt wonderful! She had promised her pupils and their instructors a holiday in honour of the opening of St. Martha's Fair, and she was gratified to find that the saint beloved of all householders had inveigled a brilliant sky for her festival. St. Martha had, presumably, worked some homely magic on Briony as well, for her head was clear, and, rather than feeling an expected sense of fatigue, she was quite looking forward to the outing.

St. Martha's Fair at Lesham had begun in the sixteenth

century as a hiring-fair for householders. Housewives in search of maidservants, farmers in search of housekeepers, hearty farmgirls in search of employment had repaired there on July 29, the feast day of Martha of Bethany. Over a long period of time, however, the emphasis had shifted. Hiring was still accomplished, of course, but the fair encompassed more. The adornments had begun simply enough with merry-go-rounds, swing boats, and gingerbread stalls, but by the beginning of the racy eighteenth century, the old bucolic atmosphere had given way to a sennight of merrymaking and innocent raillery. Players' booths had arrived: first the smaller world of pasteboard, glue, and copper wire where wooden thespians presented *The Story of the Chaste Susanna* or *The History of Solomon and the Queen of Sheba* with all the impressiveness which the miniature can bring; later the same tales writ large; later still, more frivolous fare was customary.

Mr. Biddy, it seemed, was acquainted with all of these travelling actors. As their party passed amongst the booths, the games, pedlars, jugglers, and diversions, he was constantly nodding and smiling, being plucked at or saluted by old friends. He knew the venerable bearded man, frothing at the mouth and crying out in a delirium of prophetic ecstasy, who momentarily wiped away the soap bubbles to kiss Mrs. Biddy upon the cheek and greet her husband with a sharp, indecorous jest. He knew the Moon-men or Egyptians reading the future with serious expressions, startlingly handsome with their dark eyes, crimson coats, and golden earrings. He also knew those geniuses at sleight-of-hand against whom unwary yokels pitted themselves in trying to discover the coin under the cards laid out upon the table. He spoke to the swings-man and the fire-dancer, and it became evident that he was a crony in London of the jolly confectioner whose booth dispensed eringo.

"What, sir," Biddy, open-mouthed, asked of von Ahlden, "never tasted eringo? Then, by your leave, I will treat for all so that you may carry its fame back to your own country and say to your neighbours that there is in England one thing, at any rate, which they cannot match!"

Isabella, with her particular sweet tooth, was delighted by the delicacy—eringo, the root of sea-holly candied in dark sugar whose flavour still retained the crisp tang of burning. She would, if she dared, have filled her pockets with it. Always, to the end of her days, the taste of eringo brought back to her the blue felicity of this morning, which, by a sharp dichotomy of mind, she was able to divorce from the events of the afternoon.

They moved along, still marvelling. Mrs. Biddy knew, though for once her husband did not, the beautiful wife of the seedy Frenchman who, with a sang-froid born of his own safety, exhibited his wife raising an anvil with her lustrous hair and then supporting the implement upon her breast while a trio of blacksmiths forged a horseshoe upon it with the usual heavy hammers of their trade. This much impressed Ben Barstow, who knew about such things and thought it a pity that such a handsome woman was in thrall to such a wastrel as would use her thus.

They feasted upon hot cakes and pancakes and sausages of particular pungency. They wondered at the dexterity of the tight-rope dancers and slack-wire dancers, and they were all of them delighted when the door-keeper of the menagerie refused the payment for their party, saying to Mr. Biddy, "Nay, sir, actors do not take money from one another, do we?" and allowed them in to see the "great mare of the Tartarean breed," the "man-tyger warranted to pluck the feathers from a fowl," and the hooded snakes manoeuvring up on silken ropes to the sound of an turbaned Indian's pipes.

It was all colour and music and light and noise; it was tawdry and quite exhilarating, dazzling, really, to those young enough to enjoy it; particularly for those who had for weeks been pent away from diversion and recreation in the pursuit of excellence, as had been the young ladies and

Redmond. The youth, in fact, might well have been lured away by one or another of the young doxies who smiled at him, had not Benjamin Barstow kept a close eye. It was understandable, of course, the ironmaster knew, but the occasion was hardly a proper one, what with his sister and her pupils in tow. Each time the lad's eyes appeared to be straying in such a direction, the ironmaster became, of a sudden, so friendly and withal so firm that Redmond could not resist him and was easily drawn back into the company from Hollymead.

Briony enjoyed herself as much as any, for the unbroken period of study had fallen as heavily upon her as upon the others. The only difference was that, for the first time, she had to deal not with the silliness of schoolgirls, but the awakening natures of nearly grown women. Despite her adventurous spirit, fiery Consuela Ferreblanco illustrated, with every breath, the gulf between herself and the others. All morning it had been a continual "I—I—I—." Amusing as a monkey, but capricious as a child, she flirted shamelessly with any man who would pay attention and nearly compromised poor Redmond more than once by allowing one or another gallant to believe that it was only he who stood between them and their desire of her. In the schoolmistress's view, the sooner the chit was packed off again to Cuba and Don Pepe, the better.

And now, along the central path which was the midway of the fair, came a procession. At the head of it were two trumpsters, blowing so sourly as you never yet heard, and with them drummers beating out of step with each other. Behind these came the mock-officials of the fair: the plump and red-nosed Abbot of Misrule and with him the false-mayor. Then in garb of every kind, some in cap and bells, some masked and capering, some merely with ordinary clothes turned inside out, came a motley crew of revellers, shouting and raggedly chanting a bawdy hymn to Venus. It was all very good-natured and, upon the surface, innocent, despite the naughtiness. To Briony, however, the merrymakers brought the sort of edginess that comes when chalk screams against slate or breaking glass rings too high to bear. They jangled against her perception and with unconscious disquiet she moved closer to the side of the ironmaster.

"Nay, lass," he chuckled into her ear, "they are but mummers, harmless as peascods." But Briony was not altogether sure of it. She was not given to prophecies or megrims, and the brightness of the day had not so much as slightly dimmed, yet it seemed to her she felt a sort of chill all out of keeping with the time of year.

The others of their party enjoyed the procession throughly, and Isabella, never before so picked out for attention, was delighted beyond measure when a long-nosed Scaramouche made a great sport of bending his proboscis aside enough to buss her soundly upon the cheek. She squealed and giggled without restraint, pushing him away, but not struggling very hard to keep him from repeating the outrage.

"Oh, oh!" she cried to the others. "It is just like our festival of *Fasching!*"

Anne Barstow, hanging upon the arm of the Graf von Ahlden to keep from being swept away in the press of the crowd, shrieked loudly as a grotesque old bedlame beat her escort about the head and shoulders with an inflated pig's bladder; Redmond was mightily embarrassed and discomfited as only a youth on the verge of manhood can be when a band of grotesquely painted dwarfs tried to drag him off into the flow of the procession itself. Briony, for her part, kept a tight hold upon Consuela, determined that the high-spirited girl should not give herself over to some extravagant jape and be lost to sight forevermore. She ruefully reflected later that she should have held as tenaciously to Isabella as to the Cuban schoolgirl.

Piecing the events together, it seemed that the abduction had most probably taken place while the obstreperous little men were making a great to-do about dragging Redmond into the procession. It was unlikely that they were accomplices in any way, but they had provided admirable diversion during which it must have been easy enough to accomplish an otherwise difficult objective. There had been no reason, of course, to suppose that the princess must be watched every moment. Even when the headmistress had happened to glance in that direction, it had not immediately sunk into her mind that Isabella was missing. For a few precious moments she merely looked uneasily about her in hope that the girl had merely been thrust aside by the press of the crowd, but then she clutched at von Ahlden's arm and, leaning closer, shouted into his ear.

"Where is Miss Isabella?"

He seemed ready to laugh. "She was here only a moment ago when the Scaramouche was trying to kiss her. Did you not hear her screams?"

But examination proved that she was not. She was, in fact, nowhere in sight, and the face of the count began to drain quite white. It was Barstow who, when he heard it, sprang immediately into action. The procession of rollicking mummers had at last passed by, and the crowd was closing behind them. He drew the Hollymead party together at the side of the midway.

"Miss Mitchem, I depend upon you to keep the remainder of the ladies together. Right here, do you understand me? Do not for a moment stray away. Redmond, the count, Mr. Biddy, and I will fan out and search for her. If she is alone, she cannot have gone far in this crowd, but it may be difficult to locate her even if she is quite near.

"Mr. Biddy, I expect that since you know so many people you may enlist scouts or some sort of intelligence system among your friends? I have always heard that mountebanks and gypsy people have a language of all their own; perhaps you know it and can use your knowledge now?"

However he felt about being classed among mountebanks and gypsies, the tall actor nodded emphatically. "We will have good help from that quarter. Fairground folk must keep their eyes open for a mort of reasons, you know. Someone is likely to have noticed something, even in this multitude. She'll not get far."

But a sinking feeling told Briony that it was not merely a case of a thoughtless girl wanderng off on her own; even a foreigner such as Isabella would not be so simple as all that. Her mind flew once more to the still unidentified intruder skulking in the thicket at the edge of the Hollymead park and, again, she wondered about the footsteps she fancied she had heard in the corridor which had awakened her in the night. Inquiry had determined that it was not another midnight raid upon the pantry, and she had been foolish not to carry the matter further. Now she wished with all her heart that she had done.

Anne and Consuela drew together nervously, and Mrs. Biddy squeezed Briony's forearm in a gesture of reassurance. "Don't you fret, m'love. They'll find her quick enough. Mr. Biddy knows about everyone in the business, you see, and he is very popular. If anyone has seen aught of the girl, he'll know it quick enough! Fair-folk is bright-eyed, you know. They have to be; and they take notice of small things others are like to miss. Don't you fret; it will all come right."

But despite her comforting words, the day had gone dark for Briony Mitchem, gone as dull as if a heavy storm cloud had sailed asudden from nowhere to blot out the brilliant sunshine.

═ 16 ═

THE INITIAL SEARCH had proved fruitless, and Briony was furious with herself for, in her mind, a schoolmistress who allows a charge to be carried off before her very eyes has very little right to be out in the world. She felt herself to be simple-minded and naive; too unimaginative by far for her years. Benjamin Barstow, returning from the quest, had brought the sad news.

"She seems to have vanished like smoke into the air. One moment she was with us and the next she was gone. I believed, first off, that it were simply a case of a young lass trying her wings, that she would drift back as easily as she went. But I do not see how it was possible for her to vanish so completely, if it were the case. I fear for her now, I do." He took his daughter protectively into his embrace as if he could save her from a like fate.

Anne buried her face against his broad chest. "Oh, sir, what will become of her?"

Some part of his mind approvingly noted that even in such a stressful time, she retained her newly learned way of speaking. It wryly amused him and, for some reason, made her dearer than before. He patted her shoulder and stroked her lovely dark hair.

"Never you mind, lass. We'll find her all right. We have the advantage in Mr. Biddy, you see, since he has such a wide acquaintance among the fair-folk.

"The thing to do now is to find a place where you ladies can wait without being accosted and one that can serve as a central rallying-point as well. I have found an inn across the way there that seems to be both clean and respectable. If you will all come there with me, we will hire a chamber where you can rest and collect yourselves while I go on with the searching. If there is any luck, they'll give you a bit of refreshment as well."

"Oh," Anne wailed tremulously, "I couldn't touch a thing."

"I expect we could all do with a splash of cold water, at least," said Mrs. Biddy sensibly. Though not the superior in the group, she was undoubtedly senior in age and experience and she took charge of the little party with no demur from Briony. Even the rumbustious Miss Ferreblanco was subdued and biddable as they made their way through the crowd.

"Stay close together, if you please, ladies," counselled the ironmaster. "I doubt that the scandal will be repeated, but there seems no need to tempt fate." He wrapped his own arm about his daughter's waist as if he were afraid she too might be spirited away before he noticed she was gone. His kind heart went out to the Graf von Ahlden, for he could guess the agonies the count was undergoing.

It was said that the explicitly gory sign which swung above the door of The Queen's Head Inn represented either luckless Nan Boleyn or her sometime successor, Kate Howard, but no one really knew for certain; the lolling pate might as easily have been Mary of Scots, for the inn antedated all of them, originally having been a hostel for medieval pilgrims, profitably administered by grey-robed monks.

It was, for all its history, a pleasant enough country inn. The women were shown to a pleasant bedchamber of cream-washed walls and bright blue hangings at bed and window. It was restful after the glare of the noonday sun, but they soon found they could take little ease there. Not for a moment was one of them not pacing restlessly. From the window they could look directly out upon the field across the highway where the fair was set up, and very rarely did they stray away from it. Instead, they hung anxiously upon the view, hoping, by some miracle, to see Isabella making her way toward them, unharmed and free.

It was, however, Consuela, the least likely of all of them to be pensive, who expressed their feeling. "Oh," she said, "I feel so helpless. I almost wish it had happened, instead, to me!"

Isabella, however, was experiencing no such passive anxiety. On the contrary, she had begun to evince an interior virago that even she had not known she possessed. From the moment she had been so summarily dragged backward, a dirty hand clapped over her mouth, she had struggled unsuccessfully to regain control of her own fate. There were times when she had almost succeeded: even after having lost considerable weight, she was a large-boned girl, and it required two of them to restrain her, while a third brazened a way through the crowd. Surprisingly, no one came to her aid! Here was a situation where a well-dressed young woman was being abducted by three unkempt ruffians in the midst of two thousand people, and no one raised a hand to help. Save for a pitying glance or two, the most that was raised was a loud guffaw and the occasional bawdy suggestion.

"Bit of trouble with the wife, mate?" "Some wins 'em, some marries 'em, and some jus' drags 'em off to Clapham!" It mattered not that Clapham was a hundred miles away, it was the jest that counted. No one seemed to question whether a more sinister motive might exist than matrimonial distemper. *Ach, these English!*

The moment they had separated from the crowd and the hand over her mouth was slightly relaxed, she bit full into the flesh of it. Her captor drew it away with a howl. "Oi, I'm bleeding! She bit me clear through an' I'm bloody bleeding, ain't I? Look! Look at that! Blood, y'see!"

The older man on her other arm was gently reproachful.

" 'Ere, miss, there's no need for that, is there? I thought you was a lady?"

Isabella responded with kicks and a series of German cavalry oaths that her nurse and governesses would have been astonished to know were at her command, but the third of the ruffians held up a warning hand. "No good in all that, miss. For one thing there's none to hear you now, and for another, we none of us understand such jabbering gibberish."

The older one holding her snorted at this. "Stop yer japing, both of you louts. We has a job ter do, and we 'ad best get on with it an' get our pay." He somewhat relaxed his firm grip on Isabella's arm. "Here's the coach, then, miss. Will you get in quietly or must we use force?"

She continued to struggle violently. "Let go of me, you pocked-face wretch! I will go nowhere with you. Do you know who I am?"

"Yes, miss, we does know who you are: a runaway daughter. If you was only a nobody it wouldn't matter would it, naow? Just get into the coach, if yer please. You won't be 'armed if you do, you 'as my word for it."

But the one she had bitten had no such patience. "Oh, get on with it!" He thrust her roughly forward so that she barked her shins, and tears started to her eyes. She freed her arm from him long enough to strike out boldly before she was again restrained.

"You wait, you bitch, you'll pay for that!"

They hustled her into the dank interior of the coach, the older man still trying to calm her. "It won't be long, miss, and you'll be done wiv us. A bit of a ride to Lunnon, we returns you to your dad, catches our bit a silver, and there's an end ter it."

"My dad? My father, do you mean?" Isabella asked it curiously, knowing that her father had been dead for several years.

"Yes, miss," said the rougher one in a tone verging on ridicule, "yer poor old faa-ther, 'oo's not 'ad a decent night's sleep since you run off." He jostled her. "Give over, do. We knows a runaway doxy when we sees one. We've brought 'ome a plenty of 'em. What a fool you was ter go t' the fair an' be caught so easy."

That drew her up a bit. "How did you know I was going to the fair?"

" 'Ere, that'll be enough of that. We knew, miss, and that is all. They is no reason, surely, for you knowing our methods."

"Unless you is going into the snatching line yerself, eh?" crowed the other somewhat more amiably. He had taken the seat beside her, the older man opposite, and he stretched out his legs to rest his dirty boots beside his companion. "Cor," he sighed, "I'll be glad ter be back wivvin sound o' Bow Bells. A fortnight in the country is mor'n enough for me."

She was well trapped between them, and there seemed to be no present help for it. At last Isabella relented enough to rest her head against the back of the seat, trying to clear her mind, trying to marshal her thoughts, and find some way to deliver herself from this predicament. It seemed obvious to her that these men were merely what they seemed to be, cony-catchers who had no further interest in her beyond the money they would receive. For the moment she fancied she was quite safe with them, for they would not likely be rewarded for delivering injured goods. No, whatever danger lay ahead, it would come at her destination. She had best rest and prepare herself for whatever surprises lay ahead. But certain questions still paraded back and forth within her head. Who was this mysterious "dad" to whom they were carrying her? To what unknown fate was she being delivered?

The coach was closed and dim, despite the warmth of the day. The men scarcely spoke to each other or to her, and the dreary monotony of the jogging ride lulled her senses. Try as she would she could not keep the lids of her eyes from drooping. They grew heavier and heavier and, though she occasionally lifted them for a blurring glance about the fetid box in which she rode, lulled by the rhythm of the horses, she drifted off to sleep. Only dimly did her mind register the fact that there was an occasional alteration of the hoof beats; a counterpoint which, had she been more alert, might have suggested that another horse and rider travelled along beside the coach, sometimes riding ahead, sometimes lagging behind.

She awoke when the vehicle at last sighed to a stop, and she sat up with a start, certain that danger threatened. She was calmed by the soothing voice of the older man, his hand lightly patting her knee.

"Na, na, girl, it is all right. We've stopped for a bit of a rest is all."

The airlessness of the coach interior made it all the more oppressive. The man beside her snorted and shook himself awake. "Are we 'ome?"

"No such luck, mate. Use yer bean. We've the better part of the night before we sights Lunnon," said the elder.

His companion groaned. "Why I was tricked inter this I'll never know."

They sat, motionless, for a quarter of an hour, then there was a tapping at the door. The old man dropped the shutter. "Yes?"

"They don't wanter giv'us a change of 'orses," the driver complained. "They says they 'as none t'spare, 'n these is about done in. What shall we do?"

"Where's 'imself got to?"

The driver shrugged. "I dunno. Drifted off."

"Can we go on 'n try at the next village?"

"T'orses might just, but I can't go on wivvout somfin in me belly. I ain't ate since morning."

There was now the sound of another horse leisurely approaching. "What's the trouble here?"

"Only a small thing, yer honour," said the older man. "They's trouble about the 'orses, and," he added contemptuously, "Nate, 'ere, feels 'is belly rumblin'."

"I am hungry too," Isabella said, leaning forward. "Where are we?"

Her companion on the seat growled, but the rider outside seemed to have heard her. "Very well," he said to the others, "we will stop here for a little. I will speak to the innkeeper myself and see if something can be arranged about the horses. It is a long way yet to London, and I have no desire to see them founder somewhere in the wilds."

"Wot abaht food, then, guv'nor?" Isabella could hear the driver whine.

"Yes, you shall have food as well." The man on the horse leaned toward the coach. Isabella could not see him, but she heard him distinctly enough. "What about you, Miss Wittelsbach? Will you give me your word not to create a disturbance?"

"I make no bargains with villains," she said haughtily.

She could almost hear the shrug in his voice. "Very well, I fear in that case you must stay hungry."

"You must eat in shifts, then," he said to the others. "One will eat at a time, two remaining with her."

He leaned close to the coach window again. "It is a long way to a London breakfast, young woman. The people here could not possibly come to your aid in any case, and disturbance would only be distressful to all of us." He waited, but she did not answer. "Come, come, miss, do not be foolish about it."

She thought of the long ride ahead and how long it had been since she had eaten. "Very well," she said reluctantly. "You have my word."

It seemed to provoke general relief all around, and it came to her that this journey, however sinister its motive, was as tedious to the others as to herself. The very ordinariness gave the situation a frightening quality it had somehow lacked before.

The door was opened and the older man stepped down, lifting his arm to help her alight. Her seat companion nudged her impatiently. "Well then, go, wench."

Isabella stepped stiffly down, almost falling. The light was already slanting across the sky, and she had no idea where they were or how far they had travelled. She looked up at the man on horseback, squinting a little to see him better. "Remember," he cautioned, "you have given your word."

She nodded. She would remember because there seemed little else to do, since she accepted the fact that there would be small chance of help here for a young woman accompanied by four strong men.

They made their way into the dingy taproom. The establishment was scarcely more than a wayside tavern, peopled by yokels who eyed the newcomers curiously, but kept their thoughts to themselves. Isabella confirmed her thought that she could not expect any help to be forthcoming here, but she instinctively looked about for a friendly face or a kindly glance. There was none.

Two of her captors accompanied her to a table, waited until she took her place, then, surprisingly, left her there alone, although they stayed nearby. Their master still lingered at the door transacting some business with Mine Host. Satisfactorily, it appeared, for each had a pleased look when they parted. The man made his way across the room, and Isabella watched his approach warily, for he was still an unknown quantity. She had no idea why she had been abducted, but it seemed evident that her person was in no danger. She felt that she was, within limits, being treated well enough. Now, for the first time, she was able truly to look at him.

He was not an imposing man, scarcely even of middle height and with a sharp, whippetlike face which, if not altogether friendly, was not hostile. He was dressed in a sober, gentlemanly fashion, unremarkable save here, where the patrons were, for the most part, in rustic smocks and drawers. Without asking her leave, he sat down at the table.

"Well," he said, "here we are—all together. I know you

must wonder why I have brought you here, your highness. I am sure that when you got out of your bed this morning, you did not expect the day to end in such a fashion."

Highness? He knew who she was then, not mere Miss Wittelsbach.

"Who are you?" she asked him. "and what have you to do with me?"

He did not so much smile as smirk at this, but it seemed to her not at all unpleasant, merely some private amusement of his own. "My name," he said, "is neither here nor there, although, if you must give me a tag, you may think of me as Mr. Gray, which is how these ruffians know me.

"As to my connexion with you, your highness, it is tenuous in the extreme. I am a mere workman hired to do a job, even as I have hired these assistants of mine, and I carry out my commission as best I can. I am bound to say that, in this case, it has been shockingly easy. I suppose the idea of providing you with no guards until a few days ago was to protect your incognito, but it proved a foolish measure in the long run, did it not? For the most part, I had free run of Hollymead House and could have taken you away at any time I chose."

The host arrived to take their instructions for supper, and Mr. Gray chose to order for them plainly but nourishingly: a savoury stew, fresh bread and country-butter and a stoup each of stale-ale, which Isabella found gave her a slight buzzing in her head. As they ate, her captor continued his converstaion with her.

"You must be aware, your highness, that you have become something of an international embarrassment. There are those who feel that your proposed marriage is beyond all limits, quite outré."

Isabella had sometimes found herself confronting that question. It had never really been clear to her why an alliance between the obscure daughter of an obscure house and the most eligible bachelor in Europe should have been considered.

"And what answer do *you* have?" she asked.

He looked rather surprised. "I? Why, none whatsoever. Such matters are far beyond my position.

"Or, indeed, capabilities," he added modestly after a moment's thought. "I leave such worriesome matters to other heads."

They sat awhile in silence, eating the stew and, perhaps, reflecting upon their situation. She found it odd in the extreme that she should no longer feel any personal outrage at this situation in which she found herself. Perhaps it was a result of her upbringing: from earliest childhood, her life had never truly been her own. It was only to be expected that the daughter of such a house would become a pawn in affairs of political intrigue. But these last few weeks had shown her something of a different life. However they had masqueraded as schooling, they had been, for her, an almost unalloyed pleasure. She had never had such attenion as at Hollymead. Never had she been able to explore the beginnings of a friendship in the way she had done in these weeks with Anne, let alone succumb to such a relationship as the one with Redmond. Isabella was clever enough to know that, in her life, Miss Mitchem's brother was nothing, but for a little while he had been a delight and something of an education in his own right.

Arousing from her thoughts, she perceived that Mr. Gray was looking at her with what appeared to be a combination of sympathy and curiosity. The princess raised her aristocratic eyebrows at the flunkey. "Sir?"

"I feel obliged to overstep my purview, madam, to set your mind at rest."

"I hardly think that likely," she said, "but, pray, say what you will."

"Very well. It may seem of small comfort to you, but all this is for your own good. There are people who feel you must be protected. Will you accept that and try to conduct yourself accordingly?"

She was almost shocked at the effrontery which asked

her to believe such a thing. "And these ruffians of yours, I suppose they are my shining knights? If you please, sir, what led you to believe that I would accept such a statement? I am young, I know, and defenseless, but I am not a fool."

"You have just illustrated why we were forced to gain your person by such an unpleasant means," Gray said sadly.

"And have you proof of what you say? I do not know you and I have no connections in England but the Graf von Ahlden." A shocking thought lodged in her mind. "Are you saying to me that the count is my enemy?"

"No, your highness, of course not. The count is a dear confidante of your mother and, I am sure, has your best interests at heart. Unfortunately, the count, too, is in a highly vulnerable position, acting, as he does, not only for Thoningen, but for friendly elements within Berengaria. There are those, you know, who wish this alliance destroyed."

"And those who do may carry letters of passport from the English, I do not doubt?"

Gray made a face. "I have only two possible proofs of my sincerity, princess. One is in the treatment you receive. If you were in grave physical danger, you would not be sitting in a tavern over your dinner, but would almost certainly be under severe restraint. Gaolers are not generally very concerned with the welfare of their prisoners.

"The other proof is this." And from within the inside pocket of his coat he drew a small object carefully wrapped in a silk handkerchief. He handed it to Isabella. "Here is my strongest proof, princess. It comes to you with love."

Unwrapping the cloth, Isabella found an exquisitely painted miniature of a beautiful young woman. "Mama!" she said in surprise. "How do you come by this, sir?"

"You recognise it, then?" Gray asked. "We were told by the sender that you would know its provenance and recall the motto."

The princess understood what he meant. Picked out in tiny diamonds along the edge of the frame were the words: *"honneur et fidelité."*

"Of course I know it," she said. "This was given by Mama to my father on the day of their marriage. It stood always on a table beside his bed."

Gray spread his hands eloquently, as if to say without words, "I rest my case."

"But you could have come by this in a dozen ways," the girl protested. "It could have been stolen."

The man nodded imperturbably. "Quite right, your highness. In the end you have only the word of a man who holds you prisoner."

The innkeeper approached the table. "The horses have been procured and made ready, sir, for whenever you choose to continue your journey."

"Yes, yes," said Gray, "we shall be moving on presently, but first I have a taste for a dessert. Something sweet, I think."

"Well, my lord, we have a fresh pie made of green apples, or a custard, or a pudding of honey and bread."

Consulting solicitously with Isabella, Mr. Gray settled for a pitcher of rambooze, a summer syllabub of milk and wine, sugar and rosewater. The landlord presented it grandly on a salver, covered by a linen napkin, which he drew back with a flourish.

"You will notice the goblets, I hope, sir," he said with a touch of pride.

Isabella saw with interest that the glasses were adorned with the Stuart rose and bud. "These must be very old," she said.

"Fifty year or more," the landlord agreed. "I knowed you would appreciate 'em. I can allus tell the quality, I can."

She sipped the beverage with pleasure. "But are you not afraid to show them?" She knew that the English government's resentment against its former rulers was strong.

"Afraid, milady? Naow, the Stuarts is dead and gone,

ain't they? We has only the Germans over us and a poor mad king, bless his soul. I prays for 'im every night."

"And so do we all," murmured Gray. Isabella wondered if he were musing on the passing of the House of Stuart and comparing it with that of Hanover. They said the old king's son, the Prince Regent, was bringing the country down about his ears like a house of cards. They said, too, that he would never be king. Was this the master that Mr. Gray served? Was this master a man to be trusted?

She looked again at the miniature of her mother and rewrapped it carefully in the silk.

=== 17 ===

THE GRAF VON AHLDEN was convinced that Isabella would not be returned to Hollymead, and he at once hired a carriage at the inn in which to make for London. To Miss Barstow he bade a farewell that was as restrained as it was sincere. Looking across her shoulder toward her father the ironmaster he said, "There is much in my life that I must regret, dear Miss Barstow, but I shall always count myself fortunate to have met you." He bent over her hand, lifted it, and gently kissed the palm.

Benjamin Barstow walked him to the carriage. "Now, now, my friend, you'll find the lass. I am sure of it."

"I hope you are correct, sir," the count answered quietly.

"And what will you be doing in London, if I may ask?"

The count smiled ruefully. "I may well be facing a firing squad. There are people there with whom I must consult. The poor princess may have become a pawn in the game of international exchange."

"Then you know where she is?" Barstow asked in surprise.

The count shook his head. "No, I do not, but I expect I will be forwarded that information within a few hours, God willing. I only hope they do not harm her." He seemed frightened at the prospect.

When von Ahlden had gone, the others returned with heavy hearts to Hollymead. Of them all, Mr. Biddy seemed most to take no rest in the matter. Perhaps it was only pride which drove him on, but he kept returning to the fair, asking over and over, searching among his acquaintances for any shred of information, however small. Only one of the fair-folk had noticed anything out of the ordinary.

"Well, you see, sir, Mr. Biddy, it was a busy time of day. I am a marchpane seller at the moment, you know, sir—pounded almonds, pistachio nuts . . ."

The usually patient Mr. Biddy urged him to "get on with it, man. What did you see?"

"I am coming to that, sir," the candyman said in an aggrieved tone. "I don't even know if it is the same young woman, you understand, but I happened to look across the shoulder of one of me customers, and I spied this handsome young piece being hustled off by three men who didn't look to be her class." He stopped to ponder this surprising event. "But you never know these days, do you, Mr. Biddy? I mean some of these young chits get themselves up quite grand, don't they?"

"Could you describe the men?" Biddy pressed.

"Well, I cannot be certain of the details, you see, sir, because I was busy with the business, wasn't I? I mean there isn't all that much time to spare for starin' abaht, is there?"

Yes, Mr. Biddy understood that.

"What I want to say is, you see, that it might have been an abduction, or it might have been a see-duction. I seem to remember a gentlemanly looking chap hanging off to one side of the others like. Sharp-faced sort of fellow, he was—very pointed in the face like one of them racing dogs, sir."

"Racing dogs?" Biddy asked.

"Yes, sir. What is it they are called—whippets, is it? Yes, the chap had a face much like one of them whippets, sir."

It was not much to go on, but it was the best Mr. Biddy had. It seemed extraordinary to him that a young woman could be snatched from a crowded fairground and no one become alarmed, but it spoke volumes concerning the mind of merrymakers: no man bent on either pleasure or profit wants to be faced with the troubles of a stranger. He returned to Hollymead with the scrap, turning it over to Mr. Barstow, who then determined to carry it on to von Ahlden in London in the hope that, fragile as it was, it might prove useful.

"Any scrap," he had said, "however small, may prove useful."

In the meantime, life continued in much the same way at Hollymead. There was no lessening of exercises for Anne Barstow, however much upset might have arisen over the missing Isabella. Anne hardly knew what to make of the count's farewell to her, but she was determined that, should she ever meet him again, she would not have lapsed into her old manners and ways.

Redmond, on the other hand, found himself plunged into a sort of accidie that tainted his every day. He could not paint, he did not sleep well, and, certainly, there was no pleasure for him in the tennis court. Knocking the ball about, even aiming it at the bull's-eye painted on the walls, was nothing without a partner against whom to test his mettle. He, too, worried for Isabella's sake.

His sister was possessed of a different sort of problem, one not connected with Isabella's abduction. She believed herself to be cherished by a man who had never spoken of it. Benjamin Barstow was, especially since Isabella's strange disappearance, very careful of his beloved daughter, but of late he had also begun to exhibit a strong regard for the schoolmistress. Because of his silence, however, Briony was left merely to guess at his intentions. She was, as well, not entirely certain of her own feelings in the matter of marriage—to Barstow or to anyone else. She had enjoyed these last years and felt a real sense of accomplishment in the slow building of Mitchem Academy. She had always thought of the school as a sort of stopgap, a way of clearing the way for Redmond and allowing him an unencumbered inheritance when he reached his majority. Sometimes, she believed without ever pinning down her opinion, the right man would come by: someone with whom she could share all of the personally precious things in her life. He would be a man whose tastes she shared, whose background, even his relations, were like her own. She needed to be among her own kind, in the world she had always known, the world that she had always found so satisfactory.

Didn't she?

It was Redmond who brought the question to the forefront by mentioning how active the ironmaster was being in the search for Isabella, as, indeed, the others knew; letters or messengers of one kind or another seemed to be arriving and going every day. Barstow had gained Briony's permission to make Hollymead the centre of his network of communication. For the purpose he had been given both a chamber of his own, an office from which to conduct his business, and a room for his secretary, a colourless and unobtrusive man named Barrish. It was a revelation to the schoolmistress, who had never guessed how complicated his business affairs must be.

"He is like Mr. Biddy in a way, isn't he?" Redmond said. "He seems to have a lead on everything in England. It must be wonderful to have a father like that."

"Would it surprise you, Mr. Mitchem," asked Anne, "to know that he also thinks very highly of you?"

"Of me?" The youth was obviously intrigued. "Whatever for? All I ever do is scribble or daub; nothing at all like him. Why, I overheard him talking to Barrish about being called into London for a conference with the president of the Board of Trade! I mean, that is smashing, isn't it?"

Anne wondered, since Redmond was so impressed with Robinson of the Board of Trade, how he would react to knowing that her father had also recently been consulted by the prime minister himself. "I believe that my father understands the need for many sorts of men in the world, you see; artists as well as businessmen."

She turned to Briony and said, with a significant look which, happily for Miss Mitchem's peace of mind, escaped her brother's attention, "My father is very fond of you, as well."

For a few brief moments, Briony was tempted to open her heart to the ironmaster's daughter, but she hesitated. Even though it would be consoling to have a confidante, it was perhaps wiser to do so when she had come to some understanding of her own feelings. As a diversion she put her attention to Consuela, who had dropped her embroidery hoop in her lap and was gazing off into the middle distance.

"What is it, my dear? You look a thousand miles away. Are you regretting, after all, that you did not set sail for Cuba?"

The child came to herself with a blink of the eyes. "Only a little, madame. I was really thinking how unfair life can sometimes be.

"It hardly seems right, you know," she went on pensively, "I have been in England for three years—three years, madame—and absolutely nothing happened to me! And, look how Isabella has been abducted after little more than a month! She has been stolen by the gypsies, I am sure, or something equally romantic."

As if an image had been called into reality by her words, the butler, coughing discreetly, asked if he might speak to Briony in the hall, where he disclosed that there were some men at the kitchen door, "*Egyptians*, I should not wonder, by the look of them. Cook is quite nervous." He said this in such a tone of disbelief that such people should have had the audacity to come to Hollymead and Briony hid a smile.

"What is it they want?" she asked. "Are they begging?"

"Begging? Oh, no, miss, though I wouldn't put it past them to help themselves to anything not fastened down. I've put John the footman to keep an eye on them. I hope I did right, miss. We've never been bothered by that sort before."

"I am sure you did exactly the right thing," said Briony soothingly. "They wanted Mr. Biddy, I expect?"

"Yes, Miss Mitchem, but we cannot locate him."

"Very well, I will see them. They may have important information concerning Miss Isabella. Show them into the back parlour."

She could hardly have scandalised the poor man more, as she could readily see by his expression. "Never mind," she said quickly. "I will come down to the kitchen."

The two men who waited near the step were handsomely dressed in velvet coats, the one in crimson, the other a rich blue, with lace at the throat and rings in their ears. She could see their horses, a splendid pair, tethered to the gatepost of the stableyard. The younger of them, a good-looking fellow with a dazzling smile, gave her an appreciative look as she came to the door.

He pulled at his forelock respectfully. "We don't mean to be of trouble, my lady," he explained. "We were looking for Mr. Biddy, you see."

She found him so ingratiating that her lips curled in a returning smile until she felt the butler's presence at her shoulder.

"Mr. Biddy seems to be out of the house at the moment," she explained. "Perhaps you would like to discuss your business with me? How can I help you?"

The other, harder-faced man spoke up. "It is we who have come to help you. It is about that girl of yours."

"We heard that Mr. Biddy was asking questions," the young Romany explained. "We may be able to tell him something about the men."

"That would be most helpful."

His dark eyes sparked. "Would it be worth something, this information?"

Now she began to see his approach to the matter. It was their business, of course, not mere altruism nor admiration for Mr. Biddy alone. "It might be," she said warily, "if I could be sure the information is genuine."

"Oh, aye, and how would you judge that?" asked the older man sulkily. "Come away, Tawno, the lady is not interested in what we have to say."

And, indeed, she might have lost them, despite the obvious desire of his young friend to please her, had she not looked past him and seen the tall actor approaching.

"Wait, here is Mr. Biddy now."

The young gypsy gave her an audacious wink. "It be hard, my lady, to know whether to be happy or sad, eh?"

The butler would have closed the door in their faces had Briony not stopped him. "Can we offer you gentlemen some refreshment as you discuss your business with Mr. Biddy?" she asked.

Even the surly elder man grudgingly brightened. "A cup of ale or cider might wash down the dust of the road," he allowed.

"I don't believe we have any ale, miss," the butler protested, but Briony assumed her best headmistress look.

"I am sure you do," she said firmly, "and some cakes, I expect would do nicely as well.

"Would they not?" she asked the young gypsy.

"They would do very well, my lady. I thank you, and my friend, he thanks you as well."

The other man now smiled at her too. "You are a kind lady. 'Luck will smile one day on you in life.' " He said the phrase as if it were a blessing—or a spell.

Biddy, joining them, looked enquiringly at the gypsies, then drew them aside. He spoke with them for a few moments, then returned to Briony. "Perhaps it is better, miss, if I speak to them alone. I know something of their ways, you see. I believe they trust me."

"Very well," she agreed, "but be certain they are brought their cakes and ale. I have promised it, and it is their due."

An amused grin passed over his long face. "I see they have got round you already. You had best go inside, miss, or I will have no bargaining with them at all."

When, three-quarters of an hour later, he sought her out,

he was still amused. "Was their information useful?" she asked.

"Yes," he said, "I have already given it to Barrish. He will forward it on to Mr. Barstow."

He hesitated for another moment, then added, "I should always have you at my side when I am dealing with such folk, miss. They have refused payment altogether. The young Rom, though, says he will marry you and give you many sons if you will be content to sleep under the sky."

"How very impertinent," Briony said, laughing, but she found she was obscurely pleased.

= 18 =

THE APARTMENT TO which Isabella found herself conveyed upon her arrival in London was not in the least unpleasant, though you would have thought it expressly designed for the detention of the better class of prisoner. The suite consisted of a well-appointed sitting-room, a sleeping-chamber and a retiring closet, as well as a most curious and ingenious anteroom which was furnished with locked doors on either side, so that the jailer, or Mr. Gray, her warder, or the giantess who came to clean and to bring Isabella's food (prettily prepared upon a tray) need never worry about the prisoner escaping while an entrance or an exit was being effected.

The view over the Thames she found to be magnificent, but the windows were far too high above the ground for any serious consideration of escape by that route. The servant woman could not have been bribed even if Isabella had had money, for she never spoke and seemed not to understand when her charge spoke to her, though it was obvious that she was not deaf. The princess tried out the large woman in several languages, but all called up an identical look of incomprehension. She appeared to *hear* the words well enough, without an ability to make sense of them. Nevertheless, Isabella continued her attempts to talk with her, if only to retain her own sanity, for the days were very long indeed.

Mr. Gray visited often, but he declined to discuss her situation except in the most general terms.

"You must appreciate, your highness, that I have my orders in this respect and I am bound to follow them."

"Do you think that I would betray you, sir?" she asked, but it was a straw-dog question and he did not condescend to answer it. Instead he prompted her to speak of her childhood in Thoningen and about her days at Hollymead.

"It was wonderful there, wonderful!" she averred. "No one ever paid me attention like that before. Miss Mitchem did not personally browbeat and badger and bully me so lovingly, but she was the driving force behind it all. I suppose it was her experience with the girls at her school. Oh, no, that is only part of it. She is a wonderful woman. You could ask Anne Barstow, or that little Cuban girl— Consuela. Ask anyone who knows her. They will tell you. She *is* a wonderful woman!"

"Will her highness permit the impertinence of a compliment?" Gray asked.

Isabella smiled. "They have not so often come my way that I can afford to pass one by." But he hesitated until she pressed him further. "Well, sir, do you mean only to titillate and then disappoint?"

Mr. Gray both frowned and smiled at once. "No, your highness. I was merely considering how to phrase it. I find I do not know how to praise your present appearance without offending by an implied comment on your past condition. It is a remarkable alteration, you know."

"And how do you know that, if I may ask?"

Mr. Gray smiled rather wryly. "You must accept my word for that. I do assure you that it is true. You have changed from a—well, you know what you were."

"*Ja,*" she laughed, "I was a fat German cow with a terrible disposition."

Gray backed off immediately. "Oh, your highness, I did not mean to—"

"Oh, faddle! I have no illusions about my past, Mr. Gray. I only hope the alteration you see may be a permanent one. I had not much encouragement in that line before.

"I do not, of course, know what the future may hold in store for me. Do you?"

He did not answer and she looked at him sharply. "Well, Mr. Gray, do you know what lies ahead for me?" Then she laughed. "But I expect you cannot tell me that either, can you?"

He shook his head. "No, your highness, I am afraid I cannot."

"Your duty to keep silent?"

"Yes, madam."

It was as though his avowal of silence created a silence between them as well. Then he stood up awkwardly. "Oh, I almost forgot that I have a gift for you."

It was a small, corded parcel upon which she leapt with shrill squeals of delight. "It is a book, is it not? I can tell by the shape of it. Oh, how kind you are! What a wonderful surprise! I have been going mad with nothing to do and nothing to read."

Mr. Gray chuckled appreciatively. "You should have told me. But now you will have some occupation, won't you? Here, let me open it. You will break your nails on the cord."

He took it from her again and, extracting a small knife from his pocket, cut the strings quickly and efficiently. "There you are," he said, offering it to her. "Do you know our old Will?"

The book was a small, Morocco-bound volume of the comedies of William Shakespeare and she greeted it as an old friend. She appreciated the knowledge that it had been chosen to lighten her spirits and she would be happy—more than happy—delighted to share her confinement with the likes of Sir Toby, Malvolio, Rosalind, or even the two Dromios.

"I truly thank you, sir," she said, making her bob in the manner approved by Mr. Biddy. "Now, if I could only be allowed to walk about for a little time each day? Surely that giantess who tends me would be proof against my running away."

"You must never think of that," he warned. "Your safety is far more important just now than your need to move about."

"And so I am to remain your prisoner forever?" she asked with an edge to her voice.

He looked at her urgently. "Promise me that you will not endanger yourself by trying to escape. It will not be very much longer, I assure you."

Gaudily dressed and painted, the citizens of Breslau thronged the streets and alleys in celebration of the world-famous festival of *Mädchen-sommer*, but in the depths of the Schulenberg Palace all was silent save in the monkish chamber of the Graf von Mansdorf and, even there, the conversation among the men was hushed and secret.

"But they have succeeded in spiriting our quarry away from beneath our noses, Mansdorf," Albrecht Werner whined. "You promised us the world, but so far we have nothing but words."

Von Mansdorf sneered disparagingly at the elderly councilor. The old man had been drawn into this conspiracy for only one reason, because of his position of influence in the court, but now he was becoming rather more a drag to progress than an active member of the cabal.

"Do we even know who has her?" Fensner asked worriedly. "They are in a prime position to win support for the other side, you know. There is nothing like a beleaguered maiden to rally the support of the people. I warn you, Mansdorf, that if she is not found and dealt with, you will end up with a civil disturbance on your hands, not to say a revolution."

"You warn *me?*" the count sneered. Gone was his customary facade of geniality. Here among his co-conspirators he reigned supreme only so long as he showed no insecurity. He knew perfectly well that their alliance was so tenuous that with one mistake on his part they would all be at his throat and the endless labour he had performed for the benefit of Duke Rudolph and Berengaria would have been pointless.

"I have supplemented the agents in London with one or two others whom I trust implicitly to carry out my instructions. It should not be much longer before they show results.

"It is that damned gypsy half-breed who has her tucked away somewhere. London is an old city, full of nooks and crannies, but my men are thorough and know their business. They will find her, and, believe me, gentlemen, our troubles will be over. I assure you, this is no time for whining cowardice. The end is still far away. I daresay, in fact, that the amusing parts of the farce are only beginning."

Barstow and the Graf von Ahlden, if they had not been working exactly hand in glove, had throughout all the upset nevertheless been in constant communication. Barstow's mercantile connexions had proved of some value, and the leads offered them by Mr. Biddy of even more, for it developed that Mr. Gray and his friends were not altogether unknown to the widespread intelligence network upon which von Ahlden was dependent.

The Jerusalem coffeehouse, where the count and Barstow now sat to confer, served as a convenient meeting-place for many who preferred to remain anonymous. The owner, being of a secretive, Scorpion nature beneath his surface affability, was prepared, for a price, to take and dispense written messages without regard or enquiry into their content, acting as an unofficial postal drop. A number of such services were furnished here for the convenience of his patrons, some innocuous, some far less so, but all as profitable again as the dispensing of coffee and of far more importance to the men who utilised them.

Von Ahlden had drastically altered since setting forth to

London from Hollymead: his face was drawn, his complexion lifeless under its surface colour, and there was about his eyes a nervous tic which spoke of emotional weight too heavy for him to easily support. His dress was neat, but without that particular care which had always been his hallmark in those weeks past when Mr. Barstow had first made his acquaintance.

"I believe it to be almost certain that my agents have identified the culprit," the count confided. "Through Biddy's lead, we were able to move backward to the man's employer. His name appears to be Gray or, possibly, Gry, which is a common Egyptian name, and possibly how Biddy came to track him. Both may merely be aliases arising from a need for professional secrecy."

"You believe, then," asked Barstow, "that he is simply an agent working for pay?"

The count was emphatic. "Oh, undoubtedly, though who the principal or principals may be is quite another matter. I have certain suspicions but nothing to uphold them. There are factions within Berengaria, for example, which would not welcome even an ephemeral tie with this nation."

The ironmaster was confounded. "Perhaps it may be that I have failed to follow some strain of your thought, sir, but, I fear, you have left me woefully at sea."

Von Ahlden looked a little surprised. "Forgive me, Barstow. We have so much knowledge in common, that I naturally thought that your connexions . . ." He paused, and then began again. "The fact is, sir, that there are those who profess to believe that the Princess Isabella was sired not by her putative father, but by someone even more highly placed."

"An Englishman?" asked Barstow. "That would be an interesting pickle, would it not? And what randy gentleman do they pin this paternity upon?" He rocked backward upon the rear legs of his chair and chuckled. Von Ahlden's reply brought him forward with a shocked thump.

"Upon my life! You cannot mean it?" Von Ahlden

nodded conspiratorially. "You are suggesting that the Prince Regent had another daughter besides the late Princess Charlotte?"

"There may, indeed, be still another if the gossips speak truth, but that is neither here nor there, since that one is English and untitled."

"But these people do not seriously believe that Princess Isabella could be a threat to the throne? Even if it were proven that Prinny is her father, she could not succeed?"

"No, of course she could not," the count said with a smile, "though it would not be the first time that a bastard has been seated upon the throne of England."

"Then how . . . ?"

"How could it affect continental manoeuvring? In many ways, but primarily through personal politics. You may not understand the ways of European diplomacy, but I do assure you that strong undercurrents do exist. Consider, for example, that the Prince Regent was married off to his cousin Caroline of Brunswick, despite the fact that they loathed each other upon sight, because it was a profitable alliance. No, no, my friend, the marriages of ordinary folk may well be made in heaven, but those of princes are forged within the conference rooms of government."

A small, generally inconspicuous man entered the coffee-house at that moment. He paused at the door, looked about with seeming casualness, then made his way toward their table. It seemed obvious to Barstow that the chap was associated with von Ahlden, but that he was going to great lengths to occlude the knowledge of their association. He hesitated for a moment, looked about again to ensure that they were not being observed, then asked diffidently of the count, "Your lordship, may I beg a moment of your time?"

Von Ahlden looked up as if he had not previously been aware of the man's presence, though Barstow was sure that such was not the case. He glanced over at the ironmaster, seemed about to invite the man to speak before Barstow, then cautiously stood up instead.

"Pray excuse me for a moment, sir," he said. Standing a little aside, he listened to what his agent had to say. As the man murmured into the count's ear, speaking rapidly and scarcely moving his lips, a triumphant smile began to form upon his lordship's face. The man finished and crept away; von Ahlden returned to the table and threw down a coin to pay the score, quaffing the remainder of his beverage in a long swallow, then making a face at its bitterness.

He was, quite obviously, bursting with anticipation for whatever it was he was about to do; but it was equally obvious that he was not sure whether the ironmaster should be included in it.

He looked at Barstow with a considering eye, then made his decision. With an inviting gesture which drew Ben Barstow to his feet, he said, "Come along, sir. Our quarry has been run to ground, I am informed. I must be on my way, and you must come with me, for if we are to rescue the Princess Isabella, it must be now or never."

They hurried out of The Jerusalem with little regard for the interest their haste might incur, leapt into the waiting carriage that was being held by the count's informant, who had preceded them out of the building, and rode impatiently as the driver tried to cope with the slow-moving traffic. A wooden cart first blocked their way, then an ancient sedan-chair carried by men almost as old, and finally, just as they were beginning to move freely, another coach cut directly in front of them with no warning whatsoever. Despite their anxiety to be on their way, Barstow found the coachman's colourful language a wonderful thing to listen to.

"It appears," said von Ahlden as they rode, "that those who spirited the princess off were the last people one would expect it of. I confess that, all along, I have been assuming the culprits were in the pay of a certain Berengarian arch-conservative named Mansdorf, but it seems, from the information my friend here has given me, that the responsibility lies in quite another direction. I must confess that I am baffled at the motives involved and even more so at the methods employed."

Throwing off all restraint, he began to expound to the ironmaster a detailed and much-involved theory of the interlocking political intentions involved. When he had done, Benjamin Barstow was left quite silent with astonishment. He looked from one to the other of his companions and shook his head disbelievingly.

"Are you saying to me, gentlemen, that Princess Isabella has been taken into custody by the English government?"

The unobtrusive little informer shook his head violently, but left it to von Ahlden to explain. "Ah, no, my friend, would that it were that simple. If it had been done in at all an official capacity, it might be questioned in Parliament and all this underbrush which obscures the real issue cleared away. As it now stands, the poor girl is neither a guest of the country nor a prisoner. She does not, in fact, have any present existence at all."

=== 19 ===

ISABELLA HAD BECOME quite an intimate of Shakespeare's comedic characters. Sometimes she would read them aloud for company, declaiming the bright, lyrical speeches over and over until she knew them by heart. Even the maidservant seemed to appreciate the rolling cadences, for she sometimes stopped what she was doing to listen and roll her head back and forth in time to the verbal music which poured from Isabella's throat.

But it did not altogether alleviate the boredom, and there were times when Isabella stared longingly down the long drop from window to ground and mentally calculated how many sheets tied together it would require to free her. Since the maidservant removed all the bed linen when it was changed, this was idle speculation, but it exercised her mind and eased some of her frustration.

At last, midafternoon of a seemingly endless day, she heard the sound of a key rasping in the lock of the outside door, the usual pause while it was closed and locked again and then, with a marvelous tact, a rapping on the inner door. She doubted that it could be Gray, for he rarely visited in daylight, but so it proved to be. She responded politely, and the second lock was presently turned.

In his arms Mr. Gray carried a bundle or parcel, which, after his initial greeting, he presented with a gracious gesture. "This is for you, your highness. We are to pay a visit today, and it seemed to me that you might appreciate a change of wardrobe."

She opened the bundle excitedly, cheered both by the novelty and by the prospect of leavng her prison. Within was a dress of a pale green-and-silver-striped cotton, complete with underdress and shoes. With it was the lightest of sea-green cashmere shawls. Isabella could not help but murmur with apppreciation.

"You had best begin to ready yourself then," Gray advised, "since our appointment is at half past three o'clock." He drew forth a pocket watch and consulted it. "That will allow you an hour in which to dress. I shall return for you at that time."

He moved again toward the door, then hesitated, looking at her appraisingly for a moment which seemed very long. "I hope, your highness, to see you on your best behaviour today. I do assure you that the occasion warrants it."

In the hour before he returned she made herself quite ready. It had been rather difficult, she found, to dress her long hair alone, but she finally decided in favour of a simple chignon: elegant, yet effectively drawing attention to the recently revealed planes of her face. Gray, when he looked at her, showed his admiration, but he said nothing of it.

"We shall have to step along quickly," he said in a cryptic fashion, "the carriage is waiting." For the first time since she had known him (only a matter of hours altogether, she realised, but somehow it seemed longer), he seemed ill at ease, and she was on the verge of asking him if something had gone wrong, but then reflected that this was hardly the sort of question a prisoner should ask even the most pleasant of jailers. It was very peculiar that he was her abductor, her kidnapper, and even, by that act, her enemy, but he had treated her so well and, for the most part, with such courtesy, that she looked on him in quite a different way. Almost with affection, almost . . . but she shut that thought away. She wondered if, perhaps, this appointment might be as important to him as it was to her.

When they reached the passageway outside her rooms, she understood just how much of a prisoner she had been, despite the pleasant way in which she had been treated. There she saw the younger of the two ruffians who had at first ridden with her inside the coach, dirty and disheveled as if he had been on guard all this while. He stood sullenly as they came out of the chambers.

"That's right, Matt," Gray said, "you had best come down with us until the lady is safely in the carriage, then wait here until we come back."

"Aow, I been 'ere for days, sir. Gissa little relief, sir. I got me own needs, if yer follows me."

Gray said nothing, but Matthew's protests dwindled into silence under the look he received. The guard followed carefully behind as Isabella and Gray descended the stairs. The girl could not help but wonder what was going through his mind, for she suspected that fancied grievances acted upon his imagination. He had always seemed to her the least trustworthy of the three, and now she felt him to be even slightly menacing. Wherever they were headed, she hoped that he was not coming along.

In this her wish was gratified: young Nate was the coachman on the box. The older man (whose name she never knew) was dressed as a footman and showed them into a carriage far cleaner and smarter than the hack in which they had travelled to London, then clambered up behind. Gray leaned out of the window for one last admonition to Matthew, but the surly fellow was already gone, with the door slamming loudly upon his back.

They rode along in silence, Gray staring abstractedly out of the window. Isabella watched him with a certain sympathy. Her incarceration, she realised, might have been much worse. She doubted, for example, that the volume of Shakespeare had been a part of the instructions he had received from his mysterious master, and he seemed in all cases to have gone out of his way to make her as comfortable as possible.

As if he had intercepted her thoughts, he turned back to her with a serious face.

"I hope I have not made your highness too unhappy," he said.

She almost laughed. "Why, no, except for the first roughness of the men, I must admit that I have not been badly treated." She paused, bit her lip, and went on. "Your motives and behaviour are a great mystery to me, Mr. Gray, but the experience has been rather more inconvenient than unpleasant."

He nodded. "I am glad." He paused, took a rather hesitant breath, and then said, "By virtue of circumstances, I have known your highness rather longer than you have known me. It has, in fact, been my task to be your shadow ever since you have been in England."

"It was you whom they almost caught at Hollymead?"

"Oh, yes," he said almost cheerfully. "My behaviour there was clumsy, I admit. I had grown rather too overconfident, I suppose. But, I do assure you, madame, that no harm was ever intended to you by me or by my master."

Of a sudden there was a stinging in Isabella's eye, and she rubbed it with her fingers, giving a little cry of annoyance.

"What is it, your highness?" Gray asked in alarm.

She laughed a little uneasily. "Only a smut that has flown in the window and found a lodging in my eye." She rubbed at it again.

Gray was all solicitude. "You must not rub it in deeper," he warned. "Pull down on the eyelid."

She did so, but to no avail. From the waistcoat pocket he took a linen handkerchief and, leaning forward, held it toward her eye. "Hold still, if you please." He spread her eyelid with his fingers and dabbed nervously. "Ah, there it is. I see it." He leaned closer, and the coach, unsettled by the condition of the London streets, jolted violently to one side. Gray was thrown further forward, Isabella toward him. It was, surely, coincidence that her face was lifted toward him and her lips pursed in a most provocative manner.

The kiss was long and satisfactory, though, when it was done, each of the participants drew back with an expression of dismay. "Oh, your highness, I did not . . ." "Oh, sir, what did . . ." The eyes met and vowed a complicity the tongue dared not speak. Involuntarily, almost, they leaned toward each other again. Their eyes closed as their lips met with a certain tremulousness.

He drew back and looked down into her face; she stared back almost defiantly, both eyes wide, a bit of pink tongue protruded from between her lips, which gave her the expression of a small child lost in wonder at a Christmas treat.

"Your eye?" he asked. She took his handkerchief from her lap, where it had fallen, and touched it to her eyelid, blinked, and drew it away, laughing a little shakily.

"The remedy seems to have been effective."

His face took on a shielded expression. "Your highness, I do not know what came over me. My behavior was hardly that of a gentleman and I ask your pardon."

Isabella laid her hand on his. "Whatever came over you swept me along with it, Mr. Gray. There is hardly need for . . ." Her words trailed off into a whisper as his head bent once more toward hers. The handkerchief in her hand fell to the floor of the coach, the discreet white coronet in its corner being trampled underfoot.

"Stand and deliver!" The two lovers sprang apart, and, with a curse, Gray leaned halfway out of the window. They were unhappily situated in a narrow street, hardly larger than an alley. In the entrance ahead stood another, bulkier coach facing forward. At its rear, pistols trained on Nate and their carriage, were two ugly-looking toughs.

"Quickly!" Gray caught Isabella's wrist and dragged her out the door of their carriage, but it was of little use. Just pulling into the street behind them was another coach, almost identical to the one ahead.

"Not much use, sir, is it?" asked their "footman," the older man. "They have you quite boxed in." He had stepped down from the rear of the carriage and moved closer to them. Isabella screamed as she saw the servant's arm lifted high, and his thin but heavy bludgeon come down on the back of Mr. Gray's skull.

Count von Ahlden drummed impatiently upon the interior wall of the calash as they drew away from the area where, his agent had assured him, the Princess Isabella was being held captive. It was a far from savoury neighborhood, dilapidated and perilously near the dockside slums. In his letter to Volkert that very morning, von Ahlden had predicted that it was a likely place to find her if they could but pinpoint the location more exactly.

They had, in fact, been investigating it for days without success, but then, this morning, his agents had come up with the necessary lead. It would prove costly, he was sure, for such information came high, but it was well worth the expense, particularly since Volkert's last orders indicated that von Mansdorf, that old arch-conservative, had succeeded in swaying a number of councillors in his direction. Only Herr Huber and Volkert, it appeared, stood between the reactionaries and the dissolution of the Thoningen alliance.

Well, now it was undoubtedly lost. In the seat opposite, the agent tried to convince him that all would mend, but he was in no mood to listen. They had found the room in which she had been confined—quite luxurious for such an apartment—a book which belonged to her, even the clothing she had been wearing when she had been spirited away from the fairground, but nothing of the princess herself. The house was deserted, though there was ample evidence that a guard had been placed before her door day and night. There was no indication where they had taken her, or, even, if she were dead or alive. He found this a great pity for, though he had not at the beginning been particularly fond of the girl, her dedicated application at Hollymead had impressed him greatly. He did not truly believe, of course, that she had actually been harmed, but it was disheartening to reflect that she might be in some sort of difficulty, even danger.

Barstow, beside him, was becoming quite tedious, as well, asking a number of rather pointed questions about the handling of the search: questions such as why an agent had not been posted to watch the house; why, in fact, a second pair of eyes had not been detailed to follow anyone going into the house or coming out of it.

"Oh, but, sir," said the man on the opposite seat, "that is what I am trying to tell you. We *have* a man to do just that. It is merely a matter of time, sir."

"But in the meantime we must merely wait?" asked the ironmaster.

The man nodded unhappily. "But it will not be long, sir. Of that I am sure."

Von Ahlden tensed. "We are slowing down." He leaned out of the window and shouted up to the coachman, "What is it? Why are we stopping?"

The man pointed with his whip. "Seems to be a bit of trouble over there, sir."

The count peered in the direction the whip was pointing. At the end of a street so narrow it could almost be called an alley he saw what appeared to be an abandoned coach, the horses standing quietly, but the doors of the conveyance standing open. As they drew nearer something further could be perceived. It was the body of a man lying face down in the street.

The coach drew up, and the three riders sprang out and hurried toward the abandoned vehicle. The Graf von Ahlden reached it first and quickly bent over the fallen man.

"Is he alive?" the ironmaster asked.

"We shall soon see." The count turned the body over and gazed curiously into the victim's face. Then he drew back with a muffled oath. *"Gott in Himmel!* It is he!"

"Who?" the ironmaster demanded. "Who is it? Is he alive?"

As if in answer the victim groaned and fluttered his eyelids. He tried to speak, but the effort was too great. He fell silent again, though his lips continued to move.

"He seems to be badly hurt," said Barstow. "We must get him to a doctor."

"Oh, a doctor? Yes, of course, we must get him to a doctor, and pray to God, sir, that he is not badly injured for he is our only hope of finding the Princess Isabella."

"What do you mean, man? Who is he?"

"I believe I can answer that, Mr. Barstow," said the agent who had been riding with them, "This man is Augustus Fitzcarick, Viscount Lantinney and the natural son of His Royal Highness, George, Prince Regent of England."

== 20 ==

THE QUESTION OF actual precedence between the old servants and those few brought from Mitchem Academy had never been adequately settled so far as pretty Polly was concerned. She made herself of use in whatever way she could and seemed to be in and about at all times: now acting as lady's maid for Miss Anne as she had sometimes done for Miss Isabella, now riding along in the trap beside the footman to perform an errand in the village for Miss Mitchem, now lending cook a willing hand as she had done for her old mentor, Mrs. Travers, and, in this instance, flying across the entrance hall to answer the imperative knocking upon the front door merely because no one else was about.

It must be remembered that Polly was still a relatively young girl, despite the belief that servants often reach their years of maturity far more quickly than their masters, and remember as well, if you please, that, though she had been as far afield as London itself, her experience of the world was far from wide. Nevertheless, upon opening the door, she found herself confronted with the handsomest man she had ever seen, even in her dreams. He was well over six feet in height, broad-shouldered but slim-hipped with a lean, muscular frame and a flat stomach. His hair was shiny and black and curled in little tendrils about his ears and collar; his eyes were dark and velvety soft and, below his narrow moustache, he flashed a smiling appreciation of her trim figure and pretty face.

Beside this god-like creature stood a stout woman of middle age. She was dressed in an unrelieved black, which must have been vastly uncomfortable on such a warm day as this. She wore, also, an expression that could have been chiselled from stone, so severe and unrelenting did it appear. When she looked at Polly, the maidservant felt that she had been weighed in the balance and quite possibly found wanting.

The gentleman bowed, not something that often happened to the likes of Polly. "Good afternoon, señorita. I have come to consult with"—he consulted a paper in his hand—"with Miss Briony Mitchem."

"Is Miss Mitchem expecting you, sir?"

The smile flashed at her again. "I daresay she may be expecting us, but not at this specific time." He had as ingratiating a manner as Polly had ever been exposed to, and she felt a warm blush rising to her cheeks. The austere lady beside him pointedly cleared her throat, and he at once returned to a more formal mode.

"This lady is Señora Emilia Vargas," he said, "and I am . . ."

"Oh, I can guess, sir," Polly burst in enthusiastically, "you must, then, be. . ."

"Don Pedro Rodriguez, at your service," and his eyes crinkled as the smile returned to the dark face.

Señora Emilia, however, unbent not in the slightest, and Polly feared that Miss Consuela, when she had to face the dragon, might come away with slightly singed eyebrows. She asked them to come into the entry hall while she announced their arrival and presently returned to escort them to the library, where Briony had been working.

The headmistress rose as her guests came into the room; she nodded to Don Pedro, but came forward to the duenna with hands outstretched. "Ah, Señora Vargas," she said compassionately, "I fear you have been put to a great deal of worry and trouble by a thoughtless girl. I hope you will find it in your heart to forgive her?"

The lady inclined her head somewhat stiffly, but a close observer might have seen that her expression lightened in just the slightest amount. It was immediately obvious to her that no part of the fault could lie with this charming Englishwoman. "I hope the child is unharmed by her escapade."

"Oh, she is quite well for the most part, though I expect you will find her much chagrined at her behaviour. She has rather boxed herself into a corner; I hope you will not be too unrelenting in allowing her to get out."

Don Pepe too found the headmistress completely charming. He bent low over her hand and murmured something in lilting Spanish which Briony did not understand, but which brought a small smile of agreement to the duenna's face. Seeing that his hostess had no understanding of his words, he repeated them in her own language.

"I said, señorita, that it has surely been worth the extra journey to be privileged to meet such a lovely woman."

Even allowing for a degree of courtly extravagance, it was a pretty compliment, and Briony felt a warm blush rising to her cheeks. "I am happy," she replied, "that Mrs. Travers was able to direct you to us. I sent her a message, of course, as soon as Consuela arrived here, instructing her to do so should you arrive there. I confess I did not know what other action to take, señora, since I had no way of reaching you, and I knew that a letter to Consuela's father was likely to take weeks." She spread her hands in a gesture of relief. "I am happy that you have arrived to absolve me of the responsibility."

There was a light tapping at the door, and at Briony's, "Come in, please," young Consuela Ferreblanco entered the room.

"You sent for me, madame?" she asked and then saw the black figure of the señora and drew back with a little intake of breath. The duenna, for her part, stared at her charge in horror.

"Your hair!" she cried before salutations had even been

made. "Your beautiful, beautiful long black hair that was never cut from the time you were an infant, what has happened to it?"

"I cut it off, señora," said Consuela. "It was a bother."

"A bother?" moaned the señora, but Consuela's glance had gone to the startlingly handsome man who was the other occupant of the room, and her eyes grew very wide as it came to her who he must be. He made his bow to her, never letting his gaze leave her face as he did so.

"Good afternoon, Señorita Ferreblanco. I am your father's friend, Don Pepe." He mentioned nothing of the matrimonial arrangements between them. "I regret that we have not had the opportunity of meeting before now. I daresay a good deal of distress might have been avoided if I had only had the foresight to precede you to the ship."

Of a sudden, several things began to fall into place for Consuela. All her worry about being wed to a completely unknown man would have been as nothing if they had travelled together back to Cuba. It would have been almost a proper romance and courtship, with Señora Emilia there to act as a chaperone. She almost smiled at her foolishness, but then something about him, his handsomeness, his extreme self-assurance, perhaps, or that feeling he fairly radiated that he could wrap any woman in the world about his finger with a smile and a dart from those melting eyes, made her draw back in almost frantic haste. Her upper lip began to tremble, and her eyes became all awash with tears. Without even answering his salutation, she backed away and, turning, rushed from the room.

"Consuela!" Briony called after her, but the girl did not pause or look back, but hurried up the stairs and out of sight.

Don Pepe was dumbfounded. It was certainly the first time a young woman had responded to his greeting in that particular way. "What have I done?"

"I am certain it is only a matter of nerves," Briony comforted him. The duenna nodded in agreement.

"Young females are an unpredictable lot, señor, and this poor child has undergone considerable strain.

"Perhaps you will allow me to follow her, Miss Mitchem, and talk to her for a little while. She has never known a mother, you remember, and you are far too young and pretty to fill such a role. It may be one of the times when an older, more experienced woman is required."

Briony was touched and very grateful. "Indeed, señora, you may be correct. Perhaps, if we have a cup of tea—or something stronger, señor?—allowing her to settle down a little, you can then speak to her with more profit than if you follow her immediately."

She rang for refreshment and then, seeing Polly coming down the stairs, excused herself to speak to the maid-servant.

"Oh, miss, the poor thing is crying as if her heart will break. What a terrible thing must have happened. Did those folk bring her bad news?"

Briony smiled compassionately. "No, Polly, I expect that just the opposite is true. Expecting the beast, our young beauty found the prince instead, and the shock was too much for her. She is not, at the moment, sure how to respond to her good fortune. I expect she will shortly recover."

She returned to her guests. "Perhaps, señora, it will be best if you go to her now. The maidservant is much concerned about her."

Don Pepe still looked quite downcast. "It must be a difficult situation, I know, for such a lovely young thing to be asked to marry a man so much her senior. I had hoped, you see, Miss Mitchem, to have the whole of the sea voyage to win her over, but now I do not know. I had not thought I was such a terrible man, but never have I seen such an unhappy expression in the eyes of any woman."

His tone was aggrieved, as if a gross insult had been offered; perhaps, in his view, it had. They sipped the tea quietly for a number of minutes (though without much interest, the emotional climate being a touch too turbulent for the relaxation that an appreciation of the beverage requires) before he said fervently to no one in particular, though he and Briony were alone, "I never suspected how beautiful she would be! Her father never hinted that she had the face of a madonna!"

Señora Vargas was conducted by Polly to the door of Consuela's chamber, where the turbulent sobs had diminished to a steady, quiet weeping. "Should I stay with you, madame?" the maidservant asked, but the duenna waved her away.

"I believe she will better respond to one voice than to many," she answered in a whisper, "though it is thoughtful of you to enquire, my child."

Polly retreated down the corridor, and the señora tapped lightly upon the door of the room. "Consuela?" The door remained closed, but the woman rapped again, a little more loudly. "Consuela, *querida?* Consuela?"

There was still no response, but when she called another time, she believed she heard something like a strangled moan. Gently, she lifted the latch and went inside.

The shutters were closed, and the curtains were drawn so that the girl languished in darkness. The first thing Señora Vargas did was let in the air and light. She looked back at the curtained bed to see Consuela, her hair standing up in spiky tendrils, lying face down and crying as though her heart would break. When she saw that the intruder was the friendly older woman, she raised up and half-flung herself into the duenna's arms.

"Oh, señora, I have made such a fool of myself! What shall I do? Oh, *Dios*, what shall I do?"

The older woman cradled her in her arms, rocked her, petting and cooing over her until the sobs had subsided to hiccoughs, then into sighs and shuddering breaths. "It is not so terrible as you may think. What you will do, my pretty, is to rise up from your bed and wash your face in cool water. Then you will bring forth your freshest and most becoming gown . . . No, no more tears! Why are you crying now?"

"I have no clothes! They all went aboard the ship. They must be on the way to Cuba by now! This one is loaned to me by Miss Barstow." She gulped. "Mrs. Biddy cut material, but it is not done."

"Then perhaps it may be that Miss Barstow has another such frock, or Miss Mitchem or even that pretty maidservant or perhaps Mrs. Biddy has done, after all. Dear little child, do not make such obstacles of such silly things."

She stepped into the hall and softly called to Polly, explaining the situation, and the girl flew off in search of the wardrobe mistress. "I am certain she can manage something, madame. She is so clever, is Mrs. Biddy, that we all depend upon her."

The duenna went back into the sleeping chamber. "And then, when you are calmer, and your face is not quite so swollen and puffy with tears, you will go back downstairs and put all of your effort into charming the handsome Don Pepe. *Madre Dios*, if I had a chance of marrying such a man, I would trample any woman who stood in my way. He is rich and charming and as handsome as the very devil! Would you truly be stupid enough to let such a paragon slip through your fingers simply because your father, with his exquisite taste, chose the man for you because you were not in Cuba to choose him for yourself?"

Polly came hurrying back with Mrs. Biddy in tow, Anne Barstow was summoned and found in her own wardrobe a fresh and pretty muslin with puffy little sleeves and a distinctly virginal air. Consuela's face was washed, her hair smoothed as much as possible and then caught round with a wide riband of blue silk. This matched the ribbon about her waist (which was ever-so-slightly lifting the hem of her borrowed frock) and had the advantage of accentuating her sapphire-blue eyes.

"Oh, miss, you *are* a picture," Polly sighed, and both the duenna and Anne Barstow found it easy to agree.

"But that is as it may be," the señora warned. "You must overcome the impression you have made by being everything a biddable young bride should be; you must be gentle and shy and very, very innocent. Innocence counts for much with the men of our country, you know. They may love the fire, but it is innocence they marry."

In the library Don Pepe was pouring his heart out to his hostess. "Here I am, Miss Mitchem, nearly an old man of thirty-five years. I have had a full life, yes. I have had many adventures and I have been many places and seen many things, but never, never I swear, have I given my heart." He clapped his hands together in mock despair that would have been vastly amusing had he been less sincere. "I had believed my heart was ice, señorita, was stone. I had believed I must marry for business alliance, for family reasons, but that love was not for me. I believed, señorita, that Pepe Rodriguez must go through life completely alone in his soul." He paused, not at all dramatically, and looked to her for confirmation. "To go down that long pathway of life alone, Miss Mitchem, is not a good thing, do you think?"

"Oh, no, señor," Briony agreed hastily. "It is not a good thing at all, but it is sometimes difficult to find the heart's desire, is it not?"

He looked at her as if she had been the source of a heavenly revelation, as if her words were the very syllables of angelic voices made manifest. "Oh, Señorita Mitchem, how good it is to find someone who truly understands the heart of another. I knew from the moment I saw you that my little Consuela must be a wonderful creature because you have been her teacher. If her soul is at all like yours, if she has your heart, your wisdom, we shall have a long and very contented married life."

In a swift movement he was out of his chair and kneeling

at her feet. Taking her hand in his own he kissed it reverently. "I adore you, Miss Mitchem, for the promise of joy you have given to me."

From the doorway there came a horrified gasp, and, when the two turned their heads, they saw the sorry spectacle of a pretty girl in a pretty dress, with her pretty eyes swimming with tears.

She lifted her sharp little chin, however, and resolutely stilled her trembling lips. "Am I intruding, Miss Mitchem?"

Briony stood up quickly and went forward, drawing Consuela into the room. "Intruding? Not in the least, my dear. Don Pepe was merely explaining to me how much he already loved you at first sight."

The don had also arisen. "And is this true, señor?" Consuela asked as artlessly as if she expected that, if it were not, he would deny the schoolmistress's word.

He looked down at her ardently, then drew her forward and chastely kissed her forehead. "It is quite, quite true, my lovely girl. One day I hope I shall make you learn to love me too."

Consuela hesitated, sighed almost blissfully, then moved happily into his embrace.

=== 21 ===

"THE FACT IS, gentlemen," said Mr. Gray, the man they now knew by quite another name and rank, "that everything has come to ruination through my own false pride." He sighed, then put his hand to his head, as if even so little effort caused him pain. "I thought, in my ignorance, that I was a match for you, von Ahlden, and the people to whom you owe allegiance. I see that I should have taken fuller advantage of the resources at my command, instead of play-acting an adventure like a schoolboy.

"I must say, though," he added tactlessly, "that you are far more of a gentleman than I would have thought you to be, considering your masters—Mansdorf and that lot."

"My masters?" asked the count in some surprise. "I cannot imagine what you mean, sir. Surely your intelligence people have explained that I am acting under no authority but that of the Dowager Duchess of Thoningen?"

"Would that be our Isabella's mother?" asked Barstow. "I ain't so familiar with your European nobility as I expect I should be."

"Yes," said von Ahlden, "exactly. But as to your allegations, young sir, quite the contrary is true. Much of my information and some small support has come from those in Berengaria who actively oppose the machinations of von Mansdorf and his cronies. Only my knowing that you are somewhat confused by the blow you suffered prevents me from taking serious umbrage at such allegations."

They were talking together in the parlour of the rooms

Barstow always engaged when he had to be in London. The apartment suited him because it was in a commercial hotel and, like himself, plain and serviceable, giving value for money.

"Do you mean to tell me," the ironmaster asked them, "that the two of you have been working toward the same end, but in opposition to each other?" He shook his head despairingly, as if to imply that he would never understand townfolk, but he was too polite to express his reservations aloud.

"You never guessed," he asked Mr. Gray, in reality the viscount, "that the men you hired were in the pay of someone else?"

"I suppose that makes me a deuced bad judge of character," said that shamefaced gentleman.

"I daresay one might come away with that idea," the ironmaster answered dryly, "but it would seem that your heart is in the right place, for all your blundering. It may be that all is not lost. I have had my own men sniffing about with their noses to the ground. I expect we shall hear something of value before very long."

"I fear I, too, have been a great fool," von Ahlden mourned. "I thought I knew the English and English ways, but I have only succeeded in placing the princess in grave danger."

"Well, I don't know how that stands," said the viscount. "If anyone should know English ways, it is an Englishman, and I have put her in even greater danger than you. Besides which, I have developed a serious *tendre* for the lady."

Von Ahlden stared at him in open-mouthed surprise. "Do you mean to say, sir, that you have fallen in love with the Princess Isabella?"

"I fear so," said the ex-Mr. Gray miserably. "It was a foolish luxury to allow myself, but unfortunately, it is so. I was rather swept away."

"Foolish?" cried von Ahlden. "Not a bit of it!" He leapt from his chair and fairly danced about the room. "No, no, not a bit of it! Why, it could hardly be better, sir! If you truly mean what you say, it could be the solution to all of our problems."

"I should think," interposed Barstow, who guessed he had followed the count's line of reasoning well enough, "that the first thing would be to put one's hands on the young woman.

"Not literally," he hastened to add, as if what he had said might be construed as a breach of etiquette, "but a bird in the hand is worth two in the bush, eh?"

There was, at that exact moment, a growing commotion in the corridor, as if some mighty contest was being waged. The door of their parlour was thrown open roughly and a struggling young woman was thrust inside, sputtering and exploding Teutonic expletives of a kind that brought an unaccustomed flush to the cheek of the Graf von Ahlden. He was surprised, delighted, and chagrined all at once. Barstow, however, showed himself to be quietly pleased, for it was no more than he had expected from the men he employed.

"So you have found her?" he asked rhetorically.

"Oh, aye, sir, we did. 'Twas no great task from the information you and these gentlemen was able to supply us," said the wiry little man, who had accompanied the girl into the chamber. "Dealing wiv a confounded lot of ama-choors, we were. Thugs is thugs because they has no brains to be aught else, if you follow me, sir. It is a matter of applyin' wots in the noggin, ennit?"

"Yes," said Barstow, "it certainly is."

Although she was a bit disheveled, her highness seemed little the worse for wear. The state of her temper, however, was something less than felicitous. When her eyes fell upon the viscount, she began to berate him vehemently.

"You dunderhead! You great blithering English buffoon! For my own protection, you told me, for my own safety, you were hiding me away!" She took a ragged breath and tears seemed to spring involuntarily from her eyes. "I thought they had killed you!" she wailed.

"Princess . . . Isabella . . ."

She was not to be stopped. "That you should be stupid enough to get yourself killed because your masters told you to protect the princess of Schleswig-Holstein-Gundorp-Thoningen . . ."

"Isabella, I wasn't protecting the princess of Schleswig-Holstein-Gundorp-Thoningen. I was protecting the woman I care for. Trying to, anyhow," he added wryly.

"The woman you care for? Me? Not her highness, just Isabella?"

He nodded tenderly.

She shook her head angrily. "But this is useless," she said. "I am affianced to Duke Rudolph. It does not matter who else cares for me nor for whom I care."

She swung disconsolately to von Ahlden. "You, *graf*, tell him that it does not matter, that I am not allowed a heart of my own to give away."

The count's face bore an expression of discomfiture. "Please, your highness, you must believe that it was all done from the best motives."

"Whose best motives, von Ahlden?" she asked bitterly. "Not mine, I am sure."

There was a second commotion in the corridor; though quieter, the power of it was more insistent. "Make way, if you please. Make way." And the men who had delivered Princess Isabella instinctively stood aside as they recognized the buff-and-blue of the royal household. The man wearing the colours, though, had a distinctly military air. When he saw the viscount, he drew himself up to full attention and saluted smartly.

"If you please, *sir*, I have been instructed, *sir*, to remind you that you are several hours in arrears for an appointment." He clacked his heels together, took a stamping march-step in place, and added a final, "*sir!*" His saluting hand trembled theatrically at his temple and was brought down with a flourish.

The viscount looked decidedly relieved that the message was no more severe than that. "Quite right," he assented. "How did you find me?"

The household guard allowed himself a secretive smile. "We have our little ways, sir," he said in a more normal tone of voice.

"It seems that everyone does but me," the viscount said with chagrin. "Is there a conveyance below?"

The officer returned to attention. "Yes, *sir!* Two carriages at the door, *sir!*"

"Well, then," said the viscount to the others, "shall we go?"

The carriage bearing the viscount and Princess Isabella wound meanderingly through the streets, followed by the other, in which rode the remainder of the party, until it turned into an alley in Mayfair so narrow at its end that the hubs of the wheels nearly rubbed the walls on either side. The viscount, his thoughts on that other near-alley earlier in the day, found himself mildly nervous until they had moved halfway along the block and slowly come to a halt before a green-painted door in an otherwise featureless expanse of whitewashed brick wall.

His lordship did not wait until the footman leapt down from the rear, but carefully edged open the door of the carriage himself. Insinuating himself between it and the wall, he stepped down, concerned not to rub the white against his coat, and offered his arm to Isabella. As he did so, he reflected that in the hooped costume of an earlier generation such a manoeuvre might not have been possible for her to execute. It might not have even been possible for her a few months ago, he realised, but now she slipped through as smoothly as thread in a needle.

The footman, sidling between the wheels and the brick, made his way to the green door and began to knock upon it in a rhythmic fashion: one-two, one-two, one-two. At the third pair of knocks there was a scuffling sound from inside and a wooden bar was thrown back. The door opened and Isabella and the viscount stepped into a garden.

"Ah, you have come at last, have you? I was beginning to believe I had been misled by tales of your capability, young sir. What the devil has kept you so long?"

They whirled about. The gentleman hurrying toward them would have been very impressive if one had started with his glossy boots and slowly worked upward. His body was broad and powerful, his hands capable and firm, his every movement was economical and every gesture to the point. He had been dressed by some genius of a valet in a coat and nankeens which showed nary a wrinkle and, beneath his chin, his snowy stock was as high and as perfectly tied as if it had been arranged by the Beau himself. All was impressive but what sat on top, for it was the unfortunate truth that his head resembled nothing so much as a tawny pineapple from the Sandwich Islands, a circumstance delineated even further by the unruly shock of hair which rose almost vertically from the crown of his head. Isabella had never been presented to him before but she knew at once, from the caricatures and cartoons, that this could be no other than the third son of the King of England, William, the Duke of Clarence.

"Your grace, may I present her highness, Princess Isabella of Schleswig-Holstein-Gundorp-Thoningen?"

Clarence nodded impatiently. "Yes, yes, I know who she is. Your pardon, your highness, if I am brusque, but *he* has been waiting for a very long while, growing more impatient with every passing minute."

A rosy flush came across Gray's narrow whippet-face. "The traffic, sir, was execrable. London's streets are becoming disastrously congested."

A glint of humour came into the duke's eyes. "The streets of London have always been congested, my boy. I expect the Romans said exactly the same thing. I am sorry to badger you, but he has been badgering me. You know how impatient he can be."

"He, sir?" asked Isabella.

Clarence's tolerance remained, but it was obviously wearing somewhat perilously thin. He shot a quick darting look at Gray from under his heavy brows. "Do you mean to say, madam, that this young devil has told you nothing?"

"The circumstances were hardly conductive to confidences, uncle," the viscount protested. "I think the lady has taken it very well, considering."

Uncle? thought Isabella. Had she misheard?

"Humph, I suppose you are right." Clarence's encompassing look drew Isabella in. "I expect abduction is not an action to inspire confidence, is it, your highness?

"This whole affair has been badly managed from the beginning," he said, addressing Gray. Bungled, in fact." Then he relented.

"I know I need not be saying all this to you, my boy. He will doubtless ring some changes on you, and there is no necessity of going through it twice." He offered his arm to Isabella. "Come along, then. I will take you to him."

The stout man walking aimlessly along the garden paths could hardly have been unaware of their arrival, but he seemed to find the fiction of ignorance a comforting one. He was now at the far end of the garden from them, standing before a bed of prunella, gazing abstractedly at the showy heads. As she had done with his brother, Isabella recognised, from pictures she had seen, the outline of the Prince Regent of England. Mentally she began to prepare herself for the presentation.

George Augustus Frederick, created Prince of Wales and Earl of Chester and, by right of birth, Duke of Cornwall, Duke of Rothesay, Earl of Carrick and Baron Renfrew, had, at this time, been the Regent of England for some seven years. He was, she understood, King in all but name, since it was unlikely that his afflicted father would ever again regain his faculties to the point of an ability to shoulder the responsibilities of state. He had been a handsome man in his youth, this prince, but now he had grown enormously fat, often caricatured as the Prince of Whales, not Wales. Gossip said he was a libertine, a spendthrift, and a fool, and, it was true, he was both loathed and adored by his subjects in almost equal proportion. This extended, as well, to those who knew him better. His government thought him a poor thing indeed, but the intimates who moved with him on a personal basis often found him warmhearted and generous to a fault. What sort of king he would become upon his father's death was anybody's guess.

The Prince Regent's private life had not been an easy one, for he was often foolish and sometimes headstrong. Prevented by the Royal Marriage Act from taking as his wife the woman of his choice, a commoner, he had married her anyway, or gone through some ceremony, which was binding in a spiritual sense but unlawful in a temporal one. Some said the lady, Maria Fitzherbert, had even borne him a child, but that was mere conjecture, denied by all parties concerned.

However that stood, he had been forced by Parliament and his unstable father to enter a political marriage to a woman he had loathed from the first moment he saw her and never grew to tolerate. Although a daughter had come from this gross mismating with Caroline of Brunswick, this daughter had died giving birth to her own child only a year before, depriving poor Prinny of his only bodily continuance. He would one day be King of England and Hanover, but his only heir was his pineapple-domed brother. He had, the gossips said, sired other children indeed, but none who could follow him to the throne. Within a few minutes, Isabella was to bring the gossip vividly to mind.

The Prince Regent turned as he heard their approaching footsteps, and Isabella was struck by one thing alone, the kindness of his eyes and the gentle smile with which he greeted them. Contrary to what Clarence had predicted, he did not at once begin a rating of the viscount. Instead he opened his arms and drew the young man into them with every indication of affection, then he gave his attention to Isabella.

"Your Royal Highness," said Clarence, "I have the honour to present Her Highness, Isabella of Thoningen." Isabella too had heard the rumours concerning her paternity. Was she, she wondered, looking for the first time into the face of her true father? She made a deep curtsey, trying not to tremble.

His first words put her at ease. "I fear you have a grave apology due you, my dear child," he said. "Things have been done to you in the name of expediency which would be quite unforgivable in ordinary circumstances. Can you find it in your heart to forgive me for the high-handed methods I have chosen? It was really only done for your protection."

Bewildered, she looked from one face to another. "It was you, sir, who brought me here?"

He nodded. "But before you judge me, let me break to you some news I think you have not heard." He raised enquiring eyebrows to Clarence and found his belief confirmed. "The thing is, my child, what I regretfully have to say to you will be rather a shock." His face grew grave and sober. "Within the last two hours I have been the recipient of most unpleasant news."

She reached out and found the viscount's friendly hand. The Prince Regent peered at her nervously. "I do hope you are of a sanguine nature, my dear. I really have no tolerance for hysterics other than my own."

Isabella raised her chin as proudly as she had ever done. "I believe I am the inheritor of the Thoningen courage, sir."

He took his bottom lip between his teeth. Isabella irrelevantly realised for the first time that his mouth was rouged. "Ah, but that is it, you see." He gestured toward a garden bench. "Perhaps you had better sit down."

"I am quite calm, sir." His extreme hesitancy made her very uneasy.

The Prince Regent shrugged. "Very well, I suppose you know best. I have the great misfortune to advise you, Princess Isabella, that the Duchy of Thoningen no longer exists. Your neighbours were not at all pleased by the Francophile policies of your father's successor and, according to my sources, it was invaded yesterday at dawn and your cousin deposed. With the knowledge and acquiescence of the German Confederation, the Duchy of Thoningen was annexed by Berengaria." He paused, then added diffidently, "This also means, I fear, that your bridal arrangements with Duke Rudolph have also come to naught. You appear to have been deprived at one stroke of both home and fiancé."

Isabella felt the blood rushing from her face. There was a curious tingling in her hands as the world seemed suddenly to shift and lose colour. The last thing she remembered seeing was the Prince Regent's alarmed face the instant before everything in the universe turned black.

= 22 =

IN LATER YEARS the entire episode would take on a dream-like quality in Isabella's mind. As she began to recover from her faint, the first face she saw was that of the man she knew only as "Mr. Gray." He was bending solicitously over her and chafing her wrists with every evidence of alarm. The Duke of Clarence, with admirable promptness, hurried to the ornamental fountain in the center of the garden and dipped his fine lawn handkerchief, handing it to her to cool her fevered face.

The Prince Regent was in a state as distressed as her own, for when she sat up and looked about, she saw that he was running back and forth, waving his plump hands about in an agitation that might have been amusing under other circumstances. He ceased his frantic behaviour only when he saw that she was able to take a sip of the wine Clarence was now handing her.

"My mother?" Isabella asked. The Prince looked at her quite blankly for a moment.

"Your mother? Oh, yes, your mother. Well, by all reports, my dear, she has made a triumphant escape from the old palace, taking both her jewels and a substantial amount of favourite furniture." He stroked his chin and continued, musingly, "I should not wonder if your mama had not been provided with advance warning of the coup in order to set her affairs in order before the Berengarian troops arrived. It seems to me that I have heard that little love was lost between the dowager and your late papa's successor, eh?"

Isabella acknowledged this with a small smile and turned her attention back to "Mr. Gray," who was still murmuring "Oh, my dearest, oh, my dearest girl," long after she had recovered from her indisposition. He also kept lifting her fingers to his lips in a most endearing way, until the Duke of Clarence called him up rather sharply.

"Augustus, do be sensible. Her highness went into quite a proper swoon, but now she has come out of it like any healthy and sensible young woman. Pray, do not make a medical phenomenon out of it."

"Sorry, sir."

"Never mind, my boy; I daresay you come by your emotional tendencies in an honest way," the Duke said as he cast an oblique look at his brother.

The Prince Regent took no notice, but said heartily to Isabella, "You are quite recovered now, my dear? I know this has all been a remarkable shock, but your mother is well on her way to Vienna, where, I dare say, you will soon be free to join her."

But he looked rather dourly at the young viscount. "As for the indignities you have suffered at the hands of this young blockhead . . . perhaps the less said the better. The trials are over, you know, and best forgotten."

At his words something inside Isabella made an almost audible "snap!" and she felt a red bubble of fury soaring toward the surface. Standing up and supporting herself with one hand on the back of the garden seat, she stared directly into the Prince Regent's face.

"With all due respect, Your Royal Highness, I am appalled at your insensitivity! First I am kidnapped, manhandled by ruffians, then held prisoner for an age with practically no one to talk to but a maidservant who is either dumb or deficient, then captured by still another band of brigands, hauled and mauled about, and now, sir," she asked, her voice rising to a shrill pitch of anger, "you have the inconsideration to suggest that I merely sweep it all from my mind and forget it?

"This from a prince of England? This from someone whom the scandalmongers of every German court whisper might have been my father? *Mein Gott*, Your Highness, you astound me!"

The Prince Regent blinked and his pale hands fluttered. "Your father? Good Lord, I never met your mama but once and scarcely had more than a word or two with her in a public hall filled with two hundred pairs of watching eyes. Even the most dedicated roué cannot overcome a circumstance such as that, my child."

"Isabella! Papa! Please!"

The burgeoning altercation ceased immediately, leaving Isabella horribly concious of *lèse majesté*; but that was not all. She looked quickly from one to another of the three men: the pineapple-polled Duke of Clarence, the Prince Regent of England and . . .

"Papa?" she asked disbelievingly.

It was the Duke who spoke first. "Now the cast is thrown!" he declared with a worried frown. He waved a hand toward "Mr. Gray." "Your Highness, Princess Isabella, may I have the dubious honour of presenting my scapegrace nephew, Augustus Fitzcarrick, Viscount Lantinney?"

The young viscount bowed half-ironically, as if disclaiming his rank. "Can you forgive me, Isabella?" he asked.

But before she could answer, the Duke of Clarence addressed his brother in a firm tone. "If you want my view, sir, the gel is completely in the right. What was all this foolishness about in the first place, if I may ask?"

"Why, drat it, to keep her safe," Prinny blustered. "To keep her out of the hands of Mansdorf and his crew."

"Meddling in another country's affairs, in other words, eh, brother?"

"Nonsense!" said the Regent. "Nonsense! Matters of state!"

"Nevertheless, Papa," pressed the viscount, "if Isabella is not to marry Rudolph and there is no longer the question of a political alliance, may I then feel free to press *my* claim?"

His father sniffed and cleared his throat disdainfully. "Humph! I daresay you will do as you like, you young jackanapes. Heaven knows, you usually manage to do so in the end." But there was the hint of a smile lurking behind his mask of petulance. He looked at Isabella and the smile broke through like the sun from behind a cloud. "By all means ask her, sir. Damned if I might not ask her myself if I could."

Viscount Lantinney, beloved son of the so-called "First Gentleman of Europe," even though upon the wrong side of the blanket, extended his hands to the Princess Isabella. "Will you have me, Isabella?"

But the princess raised her chin in a show of great hauteur. "Certainly your request at such a time is most improper, sir. Even you must know that there are precedents and guidelines for this sort of thing. Being proffered a proposal in such a dubious manner is hardly the compliment you seem to think it.

"If you wish to marry *me*, Lord Fitzcarrick, you must first be so good as to discuss the matter with my mama in Vienna."

Then she relented and gave him a look of mischievous complicity. "I daresay, though, sir, that—all things considered—my mother might be happy to have me off her hands."

By the time von Ahlden and the ironmaster had been given entry to the garden, the viscount's father had hurried off so that he might later deny that any such meeting had ever taken place. But the Duke of Clarence remained and, once he knew who the intruders were, greeted them with great enthusiasm. Barstow he had often heard lauded as the coming man in industry, and von Ahlden, of course, was a diplomat central to this whole mix-up.

"I am sure there is something we can do to regularise your position, old chap," he told von Ahlden breezily. "Prinny will not take personal responsibility, you understand, but certain strings can be plucked to bring about a degree of harmony. This hotchpotch of Thoningen affairs is, after all, a matter for the German Federation to deal with, not jolly old England, what?"

But von Ahlden's face had gone quite choleric. "The Prince Regent, sir, has a prime connexion to the German Federation through his position as the heir of Hanover. Let us not pretend even among ourselves that his hands are entirely clean."

The Duke of Clarence all but froze him with a look. "Graf von Ahlden, my brother is the best chap alive and certainly far from the conniver you seem to think him, no matter how some tiny German duchy may be affected. I feel sure he will bear your situation in mind. I beg you, do not make yourself overwrought."

He gestured toward the lovers, now walking along the garden path. "The princess is in excellent keeping and her future seems reasonably assured, what? Would you not say so, eh?"

Barstow was wryly amused that the count had at one time believed the Regent's son to be a gypsy, but he was still not at all confident that things were as simple as they seemed. As charming as the whippet-faced youngster was, the ironmaster remained to be completely convinced that the viscount was not his father's spy; it would not be far beyond the bounds of previous Hanoverian manipulation.

What would England be like, he wondered, when mad old Farmer George passed on and the Prince Regent took his place as king?

The two men had had need, of course, to return to

Hollymead as soon as possible, and their coachman had been urged to keep them moving more quickly than was strictly comfortable or safe. As they rolled and rattled about within the carriage, Barstow more than once diffidently cleared his throat and looked askance at his companion before finally turning his thoughts into speech.

"You know, count, I could find a place for a chap like you. You need not depend upon the whims of royalty. I daresay I could even put you in funds until your own affairs are set straight. It cannot be easy to find oneself in your position, but you need not believe you are entirely without friends."

Von Ahlden turned full around, loosing his hand completely from the strap by which he was hanging on, and was almost thrown to the floor in consequence. When he had righted himself he completed the aborted gesture and Barstow took the proffered hand gracefully.

"What a fine sort you are," von Ahlden said fervently. "I have guessed it for some time, of course, but until now it has not been directed so straight at me.

"The situation, you see," he went on, "is not quite as you imagine it. My German affairs are in disarray, it is true, but I am not the penniless waif you appear to believe. I daresay I shall soon be quite right again, though I thank you for your offer. I hope, quite soon, to ask a further indulgence of you."

He did not continue to speak about the matter for a few moments. Then, as if he could delay the question no further, he asked with a serious look, "Have I your permission, sir, to seek your daughter's hand?"

"Well, I don't know about that," Barstow answered as if he had never considered the possibility. "Your world is a mort different than what she is used to. Will you make her happy? I care for little in life except that, you know."

"I care for Anne with all my heart," the count declared fervently. "More than that I cannot say."

After long hours of jolting about, they were happy at last

to find themselves at the edge of Hollymead's park, and now the coach seemed almost to fly along the drive. Barstow, looking eagerly from the window, thought that he could see two slim and graceful figures standing under the porte-cochere. He had not yet answered von Ahlden's question; now he grinned at him and made the age-old thumbs up gesture.

"If she will have you, lad, the girl is yours," he told von Ahlden, for gazing now upon the face of Briony Mitchem in the light of the lanterns as the coach pulled up, he felt that the count's answer to his question had been perhaps the best answer of all—that he cared for Anne with all his heart. Ultimately, indeed, it was the only answer which mattered a tinker's dam.

After the rush of greeting and the recitation of the news about Isabella had been exchanged for that of Consuela, von Ahlden, with a look of complicity at Barstow, took Anne into the house. Briony would have followed, but the ironmaster, clearing his throat, held her back.

"Let them have a few moments alone, my dear lady. I believe they have a thing or two to say to each other." Always a forthright man, he looked helplessly at her now. "Would you mind if you and I walked about a bit? I need to stretch my legs after the journey."

"Certainly, sir," she answered quietly. "I hope it was not too terribly tiring."

"Ah, as to that, I am more used to it than some. I travel a great deal, you know."

"Yes, I know."

The very placidity of her response seemed to confound him. He found himself in the position of having a great many things to say, but not knowing how to begin. The headmistress looked up at him expectantly.

"Er—Miss Mitchem—" he said at last.

"Yes, sir?"

"Miss Mitchem, my daughter and I hold you in a very high regard."

"I am pleased to hear that, Mr. Barstow."

"Well—more than regard, actually," he floundered. "The thing is, Miss Mitchem . . ."

"Yes, Mr. Barstow?"

"Miss Mitchem—Briony—I must ask you—will you do me the honour—that is, can I hope that you . . . ?"

Bedad, from what he could see of her face as he peered down at her through the dusk, the chit seemed almost to be laughing at him, her mouth curved up in a catlike smile. In a moment the ironmaster was smiling too.

"Drat it all, Briony, I have the notion that you know exactly what I am getting at."

"Do I, sir?" Her tone was innocent, but her eyes were not. "Then it should be no great problem to continue what you were saying."

"Bless you, Miss Mitchem, you are a capful." Then more softly, "Briony, will you marry me?"

The young woman crinkled her eyes at the bluster of his impatience, but when she answered, there was an underlying seriousness in her voice.

"Why, yes, sir, I expect I will."

Barstow, however, seemed unprepared to take "yes" for an answer. "I will do my best to make you happy. We shall be good companions, my dear, I know."

"Only companions? Only that?" she asked doubtfully.

He took her by the shoulders as if he would shake her. "See here, my girl, could you ever come to love me, do you expect?"

And now Briony was laughing no more, only smiling tremulously in perfect happiness and content.

"Why, yes, Mr. Barstow, I could. How could you ever have thought otherwise?"

If you have enjoyed this book and would like to receive details of other Walker Regency romances, please write to:

Regency Editor
Walker and Company
720 Fifth Avenue
New York, NY 10019